Do You Remember Me Now?

By

Khadine James-Ollivierre

2024

Grosvenor House
Publishing Limited

This book is published by
Grosvenor House Publishing Ltd
Link House
140 The Broadway, Tolworth, Surrey, KT6 7HT.
www.grosvenorhousepublishing.co.uk

This book is a work of fiction. Any resemblance to
people or events, past or present, is purely coincidental.

A CIP record for this book
is available from the British Library

ISBN 978-1-80381-925-9

Dedication

This book is dedicated to Georgina James and Anastasie Evans, my mother and grandmother.

Wish that you could be here for me to hand you the first copies.

Miss you both.

Love

Kiki xxx

Acknowledgements

To my friends and family that have had to wait
three years of me saying "It's coming".

Thank you for waiting.

To those that read the first few chapters years ago and
asked, "When are you sending the rest over?"
Here it is, in its completion!

Rossin and Tee, thank you for always being the
supportive older surrogate siblings when I needed it.

Jase and Reem, or should I say Lord Lewis and Reem.
Thanks for being my sounding boards and
other nerdy movie buff.

Finally, thanks Hass, for even sparking the idea for
me to do something that's my own all those years ago.

Now with that all said and done,
someone hand me a glass of punch.

Kiki

Chapter One

ALLOW ME TO INTRODUCE MYSELF

Nicole

God, the weather is horrible. I know it's July, but come on. What's with the heat?

This is one of the best cafés in the area. The breakfast I've ordered is top-notch. I have been coming here for years. They don't even ask to have my order anymore. They know exactly what I would like and how I would want it. Great customer service—

Sorry! How rude of me. My name is Nicole Murphy. I'm a detective at the Paddington police station. I'm just here trying to pass the time till I head to the station. It's my first day back after being on leave after the death of my partner, Paul.

My boss doesn't think I'm ready to come back, but to be honest, there's only so long one can look at four walls before they go crazy. Two months is more than long enough. So, after much hounding from me, he agreed to let me return to work. However, I need to have a psych evaluation because of "traumatic events".

To be honest with you, I'm fine – never felt better. But if it is going to make him happy, get him off my back and get me back in the office, I'll do what he says.

Sorry, what was that? Thank you for your condolences.

How? Did you hear about the murders that happened a few months ago? Well, Paul and I were investigating them.

Paul would always want to drive to any scene that they called us to. It didn't bother me, though, as I wasn't a big fan of driving. As we pulled up to the address, several people were standing on the pavement with their phones out, recording and taking pictures. Officers were trying to keep them calm and back behind the cordoned-off tape. As we walked past, I could hear the crowd of people having a go at the officers. I can tell you this for a fact, I don't miss those days. People shouting and swearing at you, being rude when you're only there to help.

"Don't you miss those days?" Paul asked as we walked up the stairs to the front door.

"God no, acting like a bouncer to a bunch of people trying to get into the club? I'm happy it's over." Paul and I shared a quick smile as we made our way through the communal hallway to the flat. When we got inside, I quickly scanned the open-plan living room/kitchen and took in the massive 75-inch flat-screen TV on the wall. The art deco furniture and plush décor all looked like they came from an *At Home Living* magazine.

I took a step down to walk into the room, and my feet sank into the plush carpet. All I could think of was the fact that I'd be pissed at all the people walking all over the house with their shoes on if the magnificent building were my house.

I walked over to the wall with the TV on it to have a look at the photos that were hanging up. There were a few lined paintings and black-and-white photos of people – some selfies and others full-length photographs.

A common feature in all the pictures was a lady who I guessed had to be the tenant in the property. That meant she was also the victim.

"My entire flat could fit into just this room." I turned to see that Paul was standing just behind me.

"Yeah," I answered him and looked down at his hand. "What's that?" I asked, pointing to his hand.

"Photo of the woman who lives here," he answered.

I took the photo and walked towards the glass garden doors. The garden was pitch-black, except for a few garden lights that were hanging at the far end.

I looked down at the photo and saw a young lady who could not be over 29 or 30 at the most. With her curly blond hair tied back, she had a light speckle of freckles on her cheeks, a bright pearly white smile and blue eyes.

Paul walked over to me and took the photo. "It looks like she had company last night. There are two wine glasses on the coffee table. One is empty and the other still has some left. They're going to dust it for prints."

I nodded at him as we walked from the room and headed towards the kitchen. The kitchen had every appliance that you could think of all in chrome and shining. "Our vic seems to fancy herself to be a bit of a chef by the look of all this stuff. Look at the number of cookbooks on the shelf."

"Everyone has a hobby," I answered as I moved around the kitchen, opening drawers and cupboard doors. My hands were in bright blue gloves so as not to leave prints.

"You look like you know your way around here," Paul said to me, and I realised that he had been watching me.

"A kitchen is a kitchen. Most people put things in the same place, no matter how big or small the place is." I closed the drawers and moved to go down the hallway. Paul followed me. We walked past the bathroom, where a member of the CSI team was bagging up clothes that were left on the floor.

We pushed on the door that led to the bedroom, and we could tell that there had been some sort of struggle. The bedcovers were hanging off the bed, the lamp on the right-hand bedside table was broken and on the floor, its cord was missing, and the mirror, just above the bed, had been shattered. It looked like the lady had had her head smashed against it, as there was an impact point and bloodstains.

"You want to have a stab at it, or should I?" I asked him.

"I'll go," he said. I took a step back and leaned against the door frame. I waved my hand in front of him to motion that he had the floor.

"I say our vic meets someone last night, they came back here to 'finish the night.'" He air-quoted this with a small smile on his face. "Things started fine, as we can see from the wine in the front room. They moved things into the bedroom, and from the look of it, one of them used the bathroom, hence the clothes there. Then they came back here, and things went left." I watched him walk up and down the bedroom between the foot of the bed and the built-in wardrobe.

"I think things went more than left," I said, pointing to the broken mirror.

He gave me a 'nah shit Sherlock' look as he lifted the bedcovers off the floor. "I found the missing cord to that lamp," he said.

I moved from where I was leaning and helped him lift the covers back on the bed. On the floor was the black cord from the lamp with the plug end still attached and the exposed wires from where it had been ripped from the lamp. "I'll get someone to come and bag it up."

"Detectives..." We turned to see an officer standing in the doorway. "The station says that the hospital has called and said that she's awake." We nodded our thanks, and he turned to leave.

"That's a shock that she's up already. Hopefully, she can give us a description," he said as he walked past me and out of the room.

4

"Hopefully," I answered as I took another look around the room and headed out after him.

The chilly air hit us as we made our way through the communal hallway and to the front door. The crowd on the street had dispersed, but there were still a few still hanging around. They were still asking questions to both the police and each other. We walked down the stairs and ducked under the police tape.

"God, I can't wait for it to warm up. I'm not built for this weather," Paul said as he turned up the collar on his coat and rubbed his hands together.

"It doesn't bother me; I like the cold weather."

He shook his head at me as we got in the car. "Well, you're just a special case... cold weather, black coffee, no sugar..."

I chuckled. "Whatever, let's get to the hospital before it gets too late," I said to him as we buckled ourselves in. He started the car.

Let me tell you the rest exactly as it happened...

Chapter Two

WHAT DO YOU REMEMBER?

Nicole

We drive in silence for a while until Paul remembers it is not in his character to be quiet.

"Are you okay over there?" he asks as we pull onto Harrow Road. Damn traffic.

Come on. It is almost 11 at night. Where are all these people going?

"Hello? Anyone there?" he says again.

I feel him looking at me, so I glance at him. "Yeah, sorry, what did you say?"

"Just asked if you were okay, gone quiet is all."

"I'm good, just thinking," I answer. I turn my attention back to the road.

Hurry, hurry, damn. You could have made the damn light, idiot.

We sat in silence till the light was green again.

Finally. That light took forever to change.

"What about?" he asks again. However, he sees the construction workers on the road and goes into a tirade. "Road works again.

This is ridiculous. They just dug up this damn road. Porchester Road always has some sort of issue that took months to sort out before they were at it again."

He turns to me as if just noticing that I have not said anything and repeats his question.

"Nothing really, just wandering thoughts," I answer. I take out my phone and start looking at something on it. I wish he would just be quiet. "Have a few things that I need to get done this weekend; it's going to be jam-packed."

"You are always busy or up to something. What now? You don't know how to keep still for a minute, do you? Always up to something. When do you have time to sleep?"

"What's the saying? Idle hands are the devil's workshop?" I say.

"Always with the old-school sayings. You sound like my grandmother, and I highly doubt that you can or would get into any kind of trouble."

I smile at that. Finally, we are now at the parking lot. I hate it here. You never get to park close to where you are going as well.

"Did they send the ward that she's in?" he asks as we get out of the car. "This weather isn't it, where are my gloves?"

"Here," I answer. Yeah, he had given them to me earlier. "Yeah, she's in the new building, third floor, St. Anna's wing. We might push it trying to see her. It's late," I say.

He has done nothing but talk the whole way here. I like Paul, but sometimes he asks too many questions. I want to get this over with. "I hate these places. It stinks," I say as we walk through the doors.

"It's not that bad. You just have to get used to it," he says as we get to the lift. He pushes the button to call the lift.

I shook my head. "I don't think so. I have spent more than enough time in them to know that I will never get used to the smell," I say as we step in, and I key in the floor we need to get to.

"You spent a lot of time in hospitals?" he asks. I can see him look at me in the blurred reflection of the lift wall.

Damn it. Shouldn't have said that.

THIRD FLOOR

Saved by the bell. I step out of the lift, and he follows. I feel his eyes on me, waiting for my answer.

"A little," I answer.

"How come?" he asks.

I don't answer. Inside, I pick up my pace and walk to the ward door, knocking as I get to it, and I luckily catch the attention of the nurse at the desk, who buzzes the intercom and waits for me to speak.

"Good evening. Sorry, we know it's late, but we're here from Paddington police station. You have a patient who was brought in tonight that we need to speak to." The nurse at the desk releases the door, and I pull it open as Paul catches up to me.

We walk over to the desk and show the nurse our IDs. "Sorry, we know it's late, but we need to speak to a patient who came in earlier, a certain Miss Annette Smith?" I say to the nurse.

She looks at me and then at Paul. "I'm sorry, it's late. You need to come back in the morning." None of what she said was addressed to me.

"We understand it's late, but it would be helpful for our investigation." Paul leans on the desk a little and gives her a small smile.

8

It is ridiculous. He is flirting with her. "Can we speed this up, please?"

"Like I just said, it's late, and she is more than likely resting." She looks back over to me for the first time since she let us onto the ward. Her brown eyes look me up and down, and she makes a face like a bad smell just passed under her nose.

She is a little shorter than me at about 5'5, which gives me a good two inches on her. God, if this was back in my younger years...

"Look, we will be here for 10 to 15 minutes max. We need to see her while any memory she has is still fresh. We need to see her now before someone else gets hurt. Would you like to be the reason that we weren't able to get a decent description of the person or persons that did this to her, and it happens again? I am sure you would not want that on your conscience," I say.

"Can we please just quickly pop in and speak to her? We will be in and out of there; you won't even remember we were here," Paul adds.

She looks over at Paul and smiles at him while biting her bottom lip. God, it is sickening. I look around the reception and see a whiteboard with room numbers and surnames. Ten rooms, three are empty as there's no names, James, Blake, Begum, and... Smith, room seven. Good. I take off walking down the hallway; I vaguely hear what Miss Nurse is saying as I continue walking. I hear Paul's footsteps behind me as he calls out to me as quietly as he can as it is late but loud enough that his voice still booms in the off-white hallway. They should repaint in here.

"You can't do stuff like that; you know that, right?" he says. He is really starting to get on my nerves; I need to get this interview over with.

"Look, we need to get as much info from her as soon as possible. Leaving it until tomorrow might mean she forgets important pieces of information; you can go back and finish flirting with Miss Thing if you like, and I can interview the vic—"

"One, I was not flirting with her. Two, if I was, why do you care?" He leans up against the door frame of the room.

"I don't. We have a job to do, and the sooner I get out of this place, the happier I'll be."

"You really do hate hospitals, don't you," he says.

I knock on the door without answering but can feel him looking at me.

"Come in," the lady behind the door says. Thank God for that. I push on the door, and we step in. Paul moves closer to the bed as I lean on the door and close it. She looks so small, so pale. She is almost the same colour as the hospital bed sheets.

"Sorry to bother you so late, Miss Smith, but we wanted to have a quick word with you." Paul's voice has taken on this soft tone. It is quite interesting to watch how his entire demeanour changes. He makes it seem so easy. I always find it difficult doing that. Yes, I might feel empathy or whatever feeling I have towards someone in a particular situation; however, getting that emotion across so the other person can see is always a fail. Police work probably isn't the best career to go into.

"It's fine; there were some other officers here earlier who said that someone else might pass by." She pushes herself up in the bed and rubs her neck.

"We have a few questions we would like to ask if you don't mind."

My voice shocks her a little; she might not have seen me walk in with Paul. "Where were you tonight?" Paul asks as he pulls out his little black book. Annette has a choker-like bruise around her neck; it looks sore.

"I was out with some people from work. We went to a bar in Angel."

"Do you remember the name?" She looks back at me.

"No, I don't... sorry."

"We work nearby and went for a drink after work."

"Can you give me the names of the people that you were with?"

"Maire Odell, Tina Blackwell, Tony Allen, and Darren Bishop," she answers. She winces a little and rubs her neck. "Do you remember what time you left? Did you leave with anyone?"

"I left around 8 to 8:30. I dropped my bag on the way out, someone helped me pick up my stuff; they walked out with me."

Paul really needs to hurry this along. This room is doing my head in. I never understand why they don't brighten these places up a bit. It doesn't have to be a five-star hotel, but they could at least paint over the damp patches and hang a photo or two. Instead, they have this wannabe sky-blue wall, if you want to call it that. The walls have cracks that are joining and looking like a puzzle – and a damp spot that kind of looks like an island, not sure which one.

"Thank you for all of this, Miss Smith..." he finishes.

"Call me Annette," the lady says.

"Thank you for your time, Annette," Paul repeats.

She looks at me and nods. It is funny that she has remembered there is someone else in the room other than our dear Paul. It is the first time that she has looked in my direction for more than three seconds since we walked in.

From nowhere, Paul starts to speak again. "I have a few more questions for you before we leave, Annette." I turn to him. I really thought he was rounding off. "What would you class your sexuality as being?"

"Excuse you?" The lady blinks.

I don't think she likes that question, but I want to see what Paul plans on getting out of this.

"I don't mean to offend you. I only ask because you say you left the bar with someone, and when visiting your flat, it looked as if more than a friendly encounter was possibly taking place before you were attacked. We need to know who we're looking for."

I stare at the lady. I could say for sure that the woman doesn't look like the type to take just anyone home. She is starting to look like those cartoon characters when they get angry. The blush is mixing with the bruise.

"I'm straight, not that that is any of your business. I don't think that's going to be any use to you as I don't remember."

"What do you mean, you don't remember?"

"Like I said, Detective Murphy, I don't remember." She looks embarrassed and angry.

"You say you left the bar with this person. You were comfortable enough to leave with this person, and you can't even tell us if they were male or female. Do you remember what race they were?" I say. If she had the strength to swing on me, she looks like she would.

"I believe it's time for you to leave." And there are our marching orders.

"I have a few more que—" Paul is pushing it a little.

"No, you don't. It's time for you to leave. Good night, Detectives."

"Thank you for your time. We'll leave you to rest," I say. Paul doesn't look so happy with me, but he's going to have to deal with it. We were not getting anything else out of her tonight.

"I know you wanted to get out of there, but we hadn't finished." He looks annoyed as we walk out of the ward. "We should have pushed her a little more."

"I get that, but you annoying her wasn't going to get us anywhere; we can come back tomorrow and have another try," I say, but he is mad. He storms off. Childish.

"Good night, Detectives." Flirty Nurse is back as we sign out.

Paul says, "Good night, I didn't catch your name."

Christ, Paul.

"Lynn."

"Nice to meet you, Lynn; thank you for letting us see her. Told you we'd be out of there before you knew it," he says.

I don't want to stand there while he does that. "We need to go." LOL, if they can see their faces.

"Yeah, we should be on our way; it's late, and you need to get back to your work. We'll be back if we have any more questions," Paul mumbles.

"Actually, I finish in an hour," she says, smiling.

"Lucky you... Oh, I should probably get your number in case I need to discuss anything else," Paul says.

"The number of the ward will do fine if we need to call for any reason." Get me out of this place. "Can we hurry this along, please, Detective Adams?"

He looks like I have just taken his favourite toy away. "Yeah, I'm coming, umm, thanks for this, night."

"You know there is no need for that. Of course, I want to help a good detective," the lady replies.

God, he better not complain on the way back to the station.

"You didn't seem like you planned on leaving at all. Do you want to be hanging around all night? It's late already, and I would like to see my bed before the sun comes up. You know we need to write up that statement," I say as we wait for the lifts.

They really need to sort out these lifts. Why is it taking so long?

"I didn't realise the time. Yeah, you're right actually..."

"It's not necessary that both of us write up her statement," I say.

DING THIRD FLOOR.

"Meaning?"

"Meaning... would you mind if I dipped out and left the write-up to you?" I ask, with a little smile on my face.

"Are you serious?" He stares at me.

"Come on, please? My place is just around the corner; there is no sense in me going to the station; I'll have to double back by myself."

Chapter Three

VISITING HOURS

Lynn

Finally, it's been a long shift. Can't wait to get home. "Nessa, I'm gone. Everyone is sleeping. I did my last round 20 mins ago." God, my back hurts. Hot bath ASAP.

"Sure, no problem, Lynn. Make sure you take yourself right home," Nessa says.

"Where else would I be going?"

"With that Fed that was here earlier, maybe?"

"He was good-looking, wasn't he?" I smile. Where did I put the card he gave me?

"He gave you his number, right?" Nessa asks.

"He gave me his card..."

"And? He didn't sound like he was just talking about you calling for work."

"I know. The other officer with him made it known that he would call for work."

"Detective, not officer."

God, yeah, what a bitch. I'm sure being an asshole isn't part of the job description. Let me get out of here. "Excuse me, yes, Detective. Hopefully, she was just in a mood because it's late, cause if not, honey – attitude."

Bag, coat, gloves, okay, home time. It's May, for God's sake. Why on earth is it so cold.

"You're telling me… anyway, get out of here. See you later, Lynn."

"See ya."

God, today was long. Can't wait to get home. Why is this lift taking so long? Finally. Got to call Mum in the morning, remind her about her appointment. This place gives me the creeps at night. Let me hurry and get out over here. Car's not that far. What was that? I swear there was someone there? Wow, okay, I must be seeing things now. I need to sleep. Jesus, it's so cold. The weather is a mess. The car's going to be freezing. Damn, not many people here tonight. Why do you always park on the other side of the car park when you're on the late shift? They really need to invest in more lights around here, or at least replace the ones that have died quicker. I can't wait to get home and get to bed. Where did I put those keys?

"Hi."

What the hell? "Jesus!"

"Wow, wow, sorry, hi. Didn't mean to scare you…"

"I would suggest that you don't sneak up on people if you don't want to scare them." God, I think my heart is going to come through my chest.

"Again, sorry, didn't mean to scare you. I thought you saw me coming."

"No, I didn't. Can I help you with something?"

"Yeah, I've been trying to get out of here for the last 20 minutes. I went to use the bathroom. Came out and must have got turned round. I'm trying to find the main entrance. The one that leads onto Praed Street, you know, Closer to Edgware Road?"

"The map on the wall would help you."

"The 'you are here' thing on the map's rubbed off."

For Pete's sake, let's just get this over with. You need to move out of the way if you want me to show you. "Excuse me," I say.

"Sorry."

Okay let's see. "It's right her— AWW!!"

What the hell? Did something just bite me? Was that a needle?

"Sorry about that," I hear the voice say. "Let me help you with your bag. Let's get you in the car before you end up on the floor. Here, easy, easy. I don't want you to bang your head."

Somebody must be around! Someone... please help.

"Don't panic, I'm not going to hurt you. You have something I need. Once I'm done, I'll let you go... Scout's honour," the voice says.

Chapter Four

LATE-NIGHT VISITOR

Killer

"Don't panic, I'm not going to hurt you. You have something I need. Once I'm done, I'll let you go… Scout's honour."

And just like that, she's out. No one's going to see her here. "Little advice for the future, park by the building entrance or where there's more light." Okay, let's see, where is that key card? Here we go, gonna need your jacket and cap too, if you don't mind. That's so kind of you, thank you. Out like a light. Let me make sure I've got everything. Thankfully, this bag isn't heavy. Okay, let's see: Syringe with etorphine, speculum, scalpel, jar, gloves, stethoscope. Let's put these on now.

They really should think about fixing the lighting out here; anything can happen. Let's get this over with. It's amazing how quiet these places are after a certain time. This would have been damn near impossible during the day. It would have been interesting to see if I could have pulled this off during the day, though. That would have been one for the books. Hmmm, that might be something for next time.

Thankfully, this jacket just about fits. God, it's so quiet that I can hear the motors in the vending machine and the fans in the computers. "How long is the food going to take? I'm starving."

Jesus, these security guards are a joke. What the hell is wrong with this thing, come on, come on stupid thing. Why the hell is this thing taking so long. There's nobody here.

DING

"Ground floor. Doors opening... Doors closing." A man comes into view.

"Did you see someone come in?" I can hear one of them ask.

"No," the other one responds. "You know that thing has a mind of its own. Think it's due for maintenance this week – sometime this week."

Christ, that's the security. Bet they don't even check the cameras.

"Third floor," I murmur to myself. Bet money there's no one at the nurses' station. Nope. No one. Knew it. What's the time? 12:06 am. They should have finished doing their checks if they are running on time. Let's get this over with. I can put this jacket and cap by the doorway. If it's found, they will think it's the nice lady in her car. The cleaners must have just finished doing the cleaning also. How much bleach did they use? I understand they keep the ward clean and everything, but this is a bit too much. My eyes are burning.

I wonder if she's sleeping. I won't knock that hard. Let's not unsettle her.

"Come in," I hear her tiny voice. She's up.

I slip in.

"Hello, Annette, how are you feeling? Do you mind if I shut the door?"

Click. I shut the door.

"Umm, I'm feeling a little bit better, thank you. My neck isn't hurting as much."

"Do you mind if I have a look?" She watches me walk closer.

God, her eyes are still so bright.

"The bruise still looks a little bad, though. How about your head? You hit it hard on that mirror, and I'm going to give you something to help you sleep."

"That won't be necessary. I'm sleeping fine now and—"

"Trust me, after what you've been through, I say a good night's sleep will be good for you." And just like that, she lifts her hand with the infusion drip connection to me. I can feel her eyes on me while I take the cap off the syringe and push the needle into the opening.

"That should start to work soon. Why don't you make yourself comfortable?"

She nods.

Aww, look at how she stretches and fixes herself in the bed. I sit on the bed and watch as the confusion starts to kick in.

"What are you doing? Wait, how do you know I hit my head on a mirror? Why can't I move my legs? What's happening?" And there's that panicked look.

"Don't fight it," I whisper. "If I were you, I would just go along with what's happening. Honestly. Cause you're not going to have a choice anyway." The absolute look of horror on her face is a sight to behold. Picture time. The etorphine has kicked in. No movement, just little noises, nothing loud, thankfully.

"I would love to sit and chat; however, I need to be out of here before the nurses do their next rounds. I guess by now you've worked out I'm not a doctor. We have met before, though. Any recollection? No? no worries, no one ever does." Here come the waterworks. "I'll be quick."

Chapter Five

WHERE AM I?

Jay

God, my head hurts. I feel like I've been hit on the head with a sledgehammer. My whole body feels heavy. Why can't I lift my arms! What the hell is going on? I must still be asleep; this must be a dream. Just try to calm down. It's just a dream. Wake up, Jay. Come on, you're just having a bad dream. You'll be fine once you wake up. Come on, try to move.

"You're awake, finally." Who the hell was that!?

"Don't bother yourself trying to move. You won't be able to." The voice sounds like it's moving around. I still can't see anyone. I try again to lift my head – nothing. Okay, this is beginning to feel real.

"Did you know there's a poison in pufferfish, a tetrodotoxin, that causes paralysis?" the voice says as it comes closer to me.

The sound of a chair getting scraped along the floor echoes throughout the room and comes to a stop at my right-hand side.

"A little too much in your body and you could end up losing consciousness and suffer respiratory failure, but this little beauty here is adrenalin; should keep you going." A hand holding a needle and wearing a glove comes into my line of sight.

This cannot be happening! Do something, scream, anything. There is a strong smell of perfume. I can't put my finger on when or on who, but I know I've smelt it before.

"Here's the thing, though. Neither does anything for pain."

Suddenly my face is turned to the right, and I finally see who has me here. They have a somewhat studying look on their face, like they're trying to read my thoughts.

"Please don't do this," I try to say but no sound comes out with the words.

"I am impressed. You heal quickly, no bruising." My face moves from left to right like they're looking for something, but I feel nothing. I can't even feel their hands on my face.

Think, think, this person knows you. Why don't you remember them? "You were so smooth at the bar, and when we went back to your place, Casanova at his best." The chair scrapes on the floor again as they get up and walk away.

They're now out of my eyeline. I can only hear them moving around the room, opening and closing draws and doors. I close my eyes and try to calm down. This must be a joke. This can't be happening. Who the hell is this person? Why can't I remember anything about them?

"Do you know what this is?" I open my eyes again. They're just out of sight. I focus on the thing they are holding in their hand. "This is called an eyelid speculum; surgeons use this to keep patients' eyelids from closing." I watch it being brought close to my eyes.

My eyes feel dry as the air gets to them. They've stepped away again.

I rack my brain, trying to think. Why me? What did I do?

"Did you know why some people consider the eyes the window to the soul? It's because you can't hide emotions with your eyes. We're able to control our body language to hide how we're feeling, but the eyes – the eyes always tell the truth."

They come back over and sit in the chair next to me. "I'm a little upset that you still don't remember me. It's only been about a month since we last met. You seemed so attentive, like you were taking in every little thing about me... Guess I was wrong."

There is a flash of light. A PICTURE! What the fuck?

"Doesn't matter. I'm used to it. This photograph will go nicely with the other one I have of the two of us." I hear the camera being put down onto something metal.

Music starts.

They come back into view, and the brightest pair of green eyes I've ever seen are looking at me so intensely. I want to look away, but I can't because of these things attached to my eyes. A sickening smile comes across their face.

"Do you remember me now?" I am asked as their right hand comes into view again, only this time with a scalpel.

Chapter Six

YOU'RE AWAKE AT LAST

Killer

Etorphine is a hell of a drug. I'm happy that I parked the car closer this time. The last one was a chore to get back to it.

He looks so peaceful while he sleeps. Let's see: needle, scalpel, scissors, forceps, speculum – aww damn. Where's that? Oh there! God, I have to remember not to buy this gum again. I don't like it.

Might as well have something to eat until he wakes up. I'll need to pick up some more fruits tomorrow. This is my last apple. It's going to have to do for now. I'll have something to eat when I get in.

What time is it? Where did I put his phone? You have to love facial recognition; no need for passcodes or fingerprints. People have got lazy, just pick up the phone and point it at yourself. Well, it has its uses, though. Umm, who's the best person to send a text to? What was his sister's name again? Sarah, Sonia, no Samantha, that's it. No Samantha or Sammie, there is a Sissy though. Let's have a look at her texts. BINGO! God, I hate pet names. Aww, how sweet? Dinner tomorrow with the family, yeah… you're not making that.

Text Message

Saturday 21st May 20:50pm

Hey sis, how you doing? I'm sorry but I'm not gonna make dinner tomorrow.

Saturday 21st May 20:50pm

JJ I'm good, WTH what do you mean you're not going to make it? You missed the last two!

God, she's annoying, and judging by the rest of the messages always having a go at him. Christ, woman, you have a whole family of your own. Can't you leave him in peace? I'm almost doing you a favour, well… from how I look at it anyway. How are you still not awake yet?

Saturday 21st May 20:51pm

I'm sorry I forgot, and I planned sum thing wit the boys, the tickets have already been bought. I'll pass during the week after work instead. I'm about to drive, so will chat to you later.

That's that. That's taken care of. Shouldn't be an issue till later next week.

Aww, sleeping beauty has awakened. "You're awake, finally."

I love seeing their eyes dart around; looks like the little ball in a pinball machine.

"Don't worry yourself about trying to move. You won't be able to."

Those little grunts are always so funny. What was the time again? 9:00pm Not bad. I need to get a new chair. The padding on this one is going.

"Did you know there's a poison in pufferfish, a tetrodotoxin, that causes paralysis?" He's a fighter, still trying to sit up. Wonder how long he'll last.

"A little too much in your body and you could end up losing consciousness and suffer respiratory failure, but this little beauty here is adrenalin, should keep you going." His eyes are funny, looking at me and the needle.

He is quite good-looking, shame. "Here's the thing, though. Neither does anything for pain." His beard is terrible. It feels like pricks through the gloves.

He's healed up nicely, no marks. "I am impressed. You heal quickly. There's no bruising."

Bet I can guess what you're thinking. God, those fucking eyes are just perfect. Step away, breathe. Aww, this damn chair, need to get one with wheels.

"You were so smooth at the bar, and when we went back to your place, Casanova at his best." Now look at you. You don't have a clue who's talking to you, do you? My head, where are those painkillers? Could have sworn I put them in here, close—Come on, what the hell is this damn thing caught on? How did a screw get stuck there? Never mind, need to get started.

"Do you know what this is?" That shut you up, didn't it? "This is called an eyelid speculum; surgeons use this to keep patient's eyelids from closing." Done and Done. They always look so funny like this. That didn't last long. Christ, shut up with all that noise. It's not like these hurt. Those should be a nice addition to the collection. I don't have that colour.

"Did you know some people consider the eyes the window to the soul? It's because you can't hide emotions with your eyes. We're able to control our body language to hide how we're feeling, but the eyes... the eyes always tell the truth." Quiet again?

VIBRATION

What now? Samantha again? Should have met you instead. Bet everyone would have been better off, nag. Let me turn this off.

"I'm a little upset that you still don't remember me. It's only been about a month since we last met. You seemed so attentive, like you were taking in every little thing about me. Guess I was wrong."

Just like everyone else, aren't you? Shouldn't have expected anything different. I need to order more film for this thing. Nothing beats old-school film, need to start using digital. Could do with some cool effects.

"Doesn't matter, I'm used to it, this will go nicely with the other one I have of the two of us." What's tonight's soundtrack going to be, shuffle.

The Flamingos, 'I Only Have Eyes for You'. Kind of fitting, and I haven't heard this in a while.

9:09pm, I give him 10 minutes before he needs the first shot. Got to love that first time they see the scalpel. It never gets old.

.

Chapter Seven

THE CALL

Nicole

My phone alarm chimes at exactly 6:30am. I feel it reverberate on my bedside table. 'Folsom Prison Blues' is the song that emanates from the speakers. It's one of my favourites. And I'd discovered it was so with other people.

In fact, I have just realised that it was what made my partner, Paul, like me the first time we met on an ongoing investigation not too long ago. He went on a long sermon, explaining why he loved the song. Like I gave a shit. He's such a talker. Always has been. But I don't tell him this. We all want to feel a shared connection. Don't we all. I tell him how I fell in love with the song too. A cross between half-truths and half-lies.

I like we have a shared likeness. Something like that. My phone continues chiming. 'The Folsom Prison Blues' is usually subtle and tranquil to me, but at this moment, the sudden disturbance makes me furious. I mean, I'm the one who'd activated the feature. It'd helped me so many times to be awake, to meet my colleagues in the office early. It's one of the best things that have ever happened to man. But times like this, when all I just want is to get some sleep, and this incessant fucking song gets me really pissed. I silently curse at whoever had this sick idea to create a machine that just keeps chiming in someone's ears. I just can't take it.

I groan on the bed. I'm lying on my stomach, head buried on the pillows, shaking it from side to side to quiet the noise somehow, but it doesn't help. Shoot. I curse under my breath as I roll over to my back, stretching my left hand to the bedside table, past my lamp, and then tap twice on my phone screen, and the noise stops abruptly. The silence in my room is bliss. Of course, I'm not going to get off this bed any time soon. I just toss my hand back and adjust my head on the pillow. Just a few more hours of shut-eye, and then I'm off this warm cocoon.

But the silence doesn't last long. It's shattered by Sleep Theory's 'Fallout' song. Another favourite of mine, which means it's now one of Paul's. Sometimes, I wonder if he's just trying to like everything about me. If he's saying he likes everything I like, just to get in my good graces. Not that he'd said anything beyond this. But sometimes I think he thinks we are more than the partners we are. That he's somewhat sexually attracted to me and wants nothing more than to get into my underwear. And that he just holds back because it is frowned upon by our office. I like to think that if I give him the consent, he won't hesitate to bed me as fast as he can. He has never openly flirted with me, only jokingly and in passing, but as my mum used to say, "Some things are not always plainly true."

Groaning again, I flip to my stomach and stretch my hand to the table. Grabbing the phone off the table, I turn and lie on my back and glance at the screen. Of course, it was Paul. His name is boldly written on the screen. Somehow, I feel that after I've answered this, I will be off the bed for good. This realisation causes an ebb of weariness to flutter inside me.

Another day. And possibly another murder. Tapping the screen once, I answer the call and put the phone in my ear. Paul's voice echoes immediately, "Sorry if I caught you at the wrong time."

I groan and sigh before saying, "You didn't. What's up?"

He says, "We've had multiple reports of a body."

I sniff loudly as my body starts to catch the cold that has somehow slipped into every hole in my room.

Paul says, "Police reports and body description just came in. Dead from overdose of nerve and muscle restraining drugs, they also missing their eyes."

I gather my bedsheets around me, trying to stay warm, although I know that since I'm awake, that is impossible. Somehow, my thermostat is down. I'm meant to have fixed it ages ago, but there's been too much to attend to.

I've been hounding my landlord with several phone calls to see if he could help me get it fixed, but the man seems to not want to do anything but collect rent.

Paul's voice brings me out of reverie. "Nicole. Are you still there?"

"Yeah. I heard you loud and clear. I'm just trying to think about this."

He says, "Well, thinking about it here won't help the case much."

Of course, I know that, I think. We have to view the corpses or images to get a better hang of what we're dealing with. Then I say, "But this string of murders should give us something, right? Should get us to know the kind of victims our killer likes."

"Yeah. But, so far, I don't think there is anything that can link the killers' victims. They're all random. Of different races and gender."

It's the truth. But I don't like being told this. So, I just remain silent. I'm certain there's something we're missing. We're just starting the investigation and still have so much ground to cover. Things are still yet to be clear in our eyes.

Paul says, "Also, the hospital called. There was an incident. Annette is dead..."

"How?" is the only thing I can say. "When? We just saw her last—"

"She's gone. Somehow the killer was able to get into the hospital unseen. It was after we left, so after visiting hours and late, they had more than enough time to do what they wanted."

"God!" I mutter softly under my breath.

"Yeah," Paul says, echoing my dread and anger. "God only knows what this sicko wants with their eyes," Paul continues. "Anyway, we need to head over to the hospital. Talk with the nurses and possibly doctors for any eyewitnesses. And then, we're going down to the station for some briefing with some doctor if what Mike Gerhardt from the front desk is telling me is the truth."

I sigh at this. This is going to be the beginning of many long days. I'm still trying to get my head around it. I say, "I'll meet you at the hospital then."

"Yeah," says Paul, and then he adds, "And try not to be late."

I sigh again at this and mutter under my breath, "Whatever." Before my colleague has the chance to respond to this, I cut the call, toss the phone back to the bedside table and flop back to the bed, sighing loudly now.

Chapter Eight

MONDAY MORNINGS

Paul

What the hell?

I'm still holding onto my phone. Nicole's words still echoing inside my head.

That is if I can't help it. Why the bloody hell would she say that?

I've noticed how unbothered and nonchalant Nicole has become towards the investigations we have handled together. It is as if she has other things on her mind.

At times when I catch her zoned out, she'd feign that she has a lot to think about. But I know what exactly it is I feel and see. I know deep down that she is just trying to hide a side of herself that she does not want me to see. I sometimes wonder what this could be, but I know I won't get an answer to this. There is something definitely wrong with my partner. There's something she's dealing with that I can't place a finger on. I'll wait and hope she makes it known to me.

But if she doesn't want to make me privy to this. It's alright. Everyone wants their privacy sometimes. I do too. Not everyone wants to tell their emotional pain or whatnot. But what I do not want is for her to be sluggish in an investigation that could be turning into the biggest one we've ever seen in both of our careers as detectives. I need my partner present, one hundred per cent, at all times. There is no way we can crack this case if we aren't communicating fully with each other.

I'll leave this be for now. Put it on the back burner of my mind. There are some other important things, like the briefings and the interviews with the possible eyewitness to the murder, that demand our attention.

Taking a deep breath, I toss the phone on the left side of my bed and pull my legs to the floor. I glance at my bedside alarm clock to see its neon green light showing 6:45am. God. I need to move now. I'm certain Nicole is already preparing, and I don't want to keep her waiting. Yawning, I push myself off my bed and start to make my way towards my bathroom.

Chapter Nine

A BODY FOUND

Killer

He looks like one of those Banksy paintings, just sitting there. I should have tied a balloon to his hand or the bench. Wonder who's going to find him first. Runner, dog walker, kids, or some uptight stay-at-home parent on the school run. What's the time? 7:20 am. Could be any of them, to be fair. Weather's not too bad today. So, a walk through the park would be a pleasant idea. I must give it to him; he lasted longer than the last one, who I only had to dope up twice.

I have never realised how nice this park is. A lot of coverage. Thankfully, that damn dog park isn't open yet. Here we go. This is perfect. A bunch of coffee shop mums, kids, and handbag dogs. What the hell is the point of those things? Yes, the kids. Stupid little rat-sized things that do nothing but make excessive noise. Why do parents do that? That kid is so far behind them. Anything could happen, and when it does, they end up crying on the news, talking about it all happened so quickly.

Oh, look, Fido's off his leash, having a sniff. People are so annoying sometimes. Wonder if Jay liked dogs. Oh shit! He peed on Jay. Ha! I really wish I could hear what they're saying. Is no one going to check on that kid? What the hell! I wonder if I should try getting closer. There's no one else out here. I could just get a little closer and leave before anyone else turns up.

"AAAH, OH MY GOD! SOMEONE CALL THE POLICE!"

Oh, looks like Karen has seen Jay's face. I should've got closer when I had the chance.

"Hello." There's a child at my feet.

Crap. "Hello, little one." Looks like little Timmy wandered off after all.

"What are you doing? Did you lose something? Are you playing hide and seek?" Christ, children ask a hundred questions at once.

"Why are you not with your mum?" I ask instead of answering the questions.

"She's with her friends. I don't like them. They're no fun."

I nod. "I see. You know, you really shouldn't wander off from your mum. Anything can happen; it's not safe. There are bad people around."

"I know karate. I can take care of myself. I'm a blue belt."

"Is that right? What's your name?"

The voice comes from far off. "JORDAAAN!!! Jordan, WHERE ARE YOU?"

Aww, now you notice he's not with you. "Jordan, let's get you back to your mum."

"Okay."

"Jordan, what's your mummy's name?"

"Carla."

"Carla... Carla what? What's her surname, her full name?"

"Carla James, I'm Jordan James."

Damn, have to pat myself on the back. I did a hell of a job on him. He trusts me, and it feels good. He looks so good up close in the light too.

"Jordan, what have I told you about running off?" the mother asks.

"Sorry, Mummy, I went to find a centipede near the flowers."

His mum's brow furrows. "Another centipede again? You need to leave those things alone. More to the point, what have I told you about wandering off? You're in big trouble. Why don't you ever listen? Christ!"

Why are you not keeping an eye on where he is? I think. Whatever happened to ancient motherhood. I guess the world is changing. Twentieth fucking century bitches procreating and having no idea how to look after their offspring.

"I'm sorry, Mummy." Jordan's head is lowered in apt submission, refusing to meet his mother's eyes.

"No. Sorry is not going to cut it. Not this time. I'm tired of always having to repeat myself when I'm talking to you. Why can't you just listen when I say something."

Carla is still yet to notice me. I wonder why. Even when I'm purposefully standing almost in front of Jordan. A random person is holding your son by the arm and standing in front of him, yet you're only interested in telling him off. You should have been paying attention to your child. I want to wave a hand in front of her and make myself known, but I restrain myself. I take it that she just wants to reprimand her son first before acknowledging the stranger in front of her.

Some people are like that.

"Promise me now, Jordan," Carla says with force when her son is still silent.

Jordan's voice is low as he answers. "I promise, Mum. I'm never going after centipedes."

"And you won't wander off."

Jordan only nods at this.

Carla gives an affectionate smile at this, stretches her right manicured palm to grab her son around the neck and pulls him towards her legs. Jordan puts his face on her jeans and holds himself there for some time. Her eyes flicker up to me this time. Finally, I'm a presence to behold. Now I get her attention. Tada! She smiles in that not-so-embarrassed way mothers do when their children do something that is not very pleasant in public.

"Hi. Sorry if he was bothering you, I have told him so many times not to bother people." She keeps smiling. Her emerald eyes glitter in the early sunlight. Gosh, what a lovely sight to see. Carla taps Jordan's head as she adds, "He seems to do crazy things these days." She firms her thin lips, muttering softly, "You know, kids, so rambunctious and fuelled by ADHD."

I smile and nod at this. Not responding. Sorry to break it to you, missy, but you don't get to leave your son and blame him if he acts like a child and tries to entertain himself chasing ants or whatever it was he was after. Carla says, "I'm grateful you were with him, and he didn't manage to go off too far. You never know what could happen to kids these days…"

She can't bring herself to finish whatever she's thinking. I don't offer to help. We all know what she wants to say. What she really means to say. Though I'm pretty sure she's not thinking about it. She's not really considering that her carelessness would have led to Jordan's possible injury or abduction. 21st-century mothers, right?

"Oh, sorry if I'm rambling too much. I'm not usually like this. Believe me. It's just – there's been a lot. And with him now. If I don't take care of it, I'll be so exhausted before afternoon." She catches herself again. "Sorry. I'm blabbing again. Ain't I?"

Now I offer a consoling word. "Oh, that's nothing. You've got to do what you have to do, right? So that they can be safe and all. You don't have to apologise for that. You have all the right to say it. You're a mother. You would be worried." Carla smiles warmly at this.

"You're right. Mothers all over the world have the right."

"Mummy, I need to use the toilet," Jordan says, pulling at her hand as he heads in the direction of home, I assume.

"Really?" she asks.

"Yes."

The three of us start walking out of the park. Carla regards me with a curious look. "I haven't seen you in this area before. Have you just moved here or just passing through?"

I smile at this. She's clever after all. "A little bit of everything, passing by, but quite close to the area. I don't normally come this way round the park," I answer.

She nods at this. "Thought as much. So, what brings you here."

"I was out running and met a friend. We talked for a while, and the next thing I knew, we were here. My next mission is to find some coffee."

Carla laughs. "You're a coffee fiend?"

"You got me, yeah. I feel like the day hasn't started properly if I don't have one."

"There are some really nice cafés in the area. If you head down the road and take the first left, on the other side of the road, you'll see a cute little place that's really good, and they have great pastries too."

"Really? Thanks, that's my next stop then."

Her face brightens at the thought that she's helped someone out. I turn to leave, then turn back. "Not to sound creepy or a loner, would the two of you like to come with? You can fill me in on all the haunts that are in the area..."

"Ooh, can we please, Mummy? I want hot chocolate." Jordan appears from behind her, wiping his hands on his shirt.

"We have stuff that we have to do today, sorry. Maybe some other time." Jordan looks sad and is about to start begging when she looks down at him, and his words seem to catch in his throat, so he can't say anything else. "How about we exchange numbers? We can arrange something to meet up, and I can introduce you to some of the neighbours in the area."

Exchange contacts. Wow. Never thought of that. Why didn't I think of that? I reprimand myself for losing my cool at a time such as this. "Sure," I say, patting my right denim pocket, pulling out my phone, scrolling my call icon, and waiting for her to get her phone out. We swap our devices and quickly type in our number. I give her one of the random numbers I use in my recently purchased burner phones. But I'm sure Carla has given me her number. She has given her contact details to a total stranger who just managed to get her son to her in a not-so-dangerous neighbourhood. She does not even know my name. "What's your name?" she asks.

Okay. She's catching up. Good. I like it when people have their wits about them. Makes me believe I'm dealing with smartasses and not idiots. I tell her a name, and she nods in acceptance. She goes on to explain that currently she's preparing to get to work and also make sure Jordan is well-fed before the nanny comes. I nod at this, although I couldn't care less. I don't fucking give a shit. But anything to get this woman to trust me. I'll do it.

Sirens fill the whole area now. Everyone on the street is craning their necks and scanning around, talking in hushed tones – probably asking what was going on. I guess a few people called the police and have surrounded Jay by now, a curmudgeon of boring and nosy neighbours. I see Carla's brow rise at the sound of the siren.

"What's going on?" she asks. I feign that I have no idea what the cops' arrival is for. Karen and a cluster of other voices are now in high decibels, even cracking through the klaxon of police sirens.

Carla looks like she wants to get out there and know what's going on. We stand there staring at the police cars, at the crowd of people in clusters on the street. They are all a few metres from the bridge, from the bench on which I had sat Jay. I hope no one saw me leaving him there because he or she could easily point me out. Which is why I need to leave this place. ASAP. I wouldn't want the police looking in my direction. The last thing I'll see is this agitated neighbour before I'm locked up forever. Nope, not happening. I have no intention of that happening at all.

Crap. I'm wandering off again. My mind always does this. Though, throughout the years, I've managed to get it under control. But sometimes it crops up, and I hardly know how to control it. I bid Carla good day and start to make my way out of her porch. I hear her say she hopes that whatever has happened, whoever was involved wasn't hurt. I chuckle at this and say under my breath, "You wish, honey, you wish."

Chapter Ten

WITNESS REPORT

Nicole

I make it to the hospital, luckily, in good time. My watch tells me I'm two minutes early. I pull my BMW i5 series beside Paul's Mercedes-Benz. He's sitting in his car fiddling with his iPhone, probably engrossed in his chess game. As usual. He has no idea of my arrival or is pretending he doesn't. But all the same, I tap my wheel twice, activating the horn, which echoes around the car park of the hospital.

Paul jerks at the sudden sound. His phone slips from his finger and drops to his lap. He turns, and I see fury building in his face. But when he sees it's me, it all but wipes the frown off his face.

Yeah, it's me. Your partner. I wave at him, smiling.

When he doesn't react to this, I hold up a bag of Starbucks and McDonald's I had gotten for him through my window. I see a small smile creep into his face.

I always know how to get to you. Angry freak. He laughs at me now and picks up his phone from his lap.

As I move to open the door, Paul unlocks his door and pushes it open. He's out before I am. Because I'm trying so hard to grab hold of these damn four bags of stupid confectionary. I make it outside and use my right hip and butt to close the door. Paul walks towards me and eyes the bags I'm holding. You've got to choose, man.

"Think this is mine," he says, taking one of the Starbucks bags and one of the McDonald's bags. Before I can utter a word, he's already ripping into the Starbucks bag and pulling out his coffee. Hungry beast, I think but don't say. He would not like that. He'll get offended, and then we'll get into a dangerous banter that I have no time or strength to address this morning.

Instead, I say, "So, who are we going to meet now?"

In between sips, Paul says, "Oh, it's one of the nurses. She didn't see the perp, but she heard some voices outside the victim's room."

"Why didn't she go in and find out what was wrong?"

Paul shrugs and says, "Beats me. Though when Mark pressured her, she said she had another patient she was desperately going to meet."

"Desperately," I say incredulously.

Paul shrugs again. "It's her words. Not mine."

I consider this for a moment, but I can't make heads or tails of what it meant. If the nurse had gone into the room when she heard the noise, she'd have seen the intruder, and that would have helped us immeasurably. But she didn't. Now, we're still at square one. No name. No face. And bodies piling up like a deck of cards.

I ask, "Can we meet the witness now, or do you want me to wait for you to finish this?"

Still sipping his coffee, Paul gestures to the hospital entrance, and we begin to make our way towards it.

"Don't you want to eat that?" he asks, pointing at the McDonald's bag in my hand.

I shake my head and say, "Oh, that's for the witness. Believe she hasn't had the time to go home since she's been on night shift."

Paul nods at this. "True."

We arrived inside the hospital a few seconds later. It's still a bustle of activities. Fresh patients wheeled in, nurses scrambling to help the ambulance team, and doctors coming out of their offices to guide them. No one glances at us. We make our way to the lifts, wait and take them to the third floor, just like we did the other night. I press the buzzer to the ward, and we wait to be let in. We head to the reception desk and meet a nurse called Nessa, going over some documents on her desk. The pretty blonde notes our presence and looks up from her paper. As usual, Paul takes the lead on this, and I let him. Some things are not worth fighting for.

"Hi, it's us again, the detectives from Paddington police station. We're here to see the nurse who found Annette Smith." Nessa nods at this, her face turning grim. At least she is not as flirty as the nurse from yesterday.

"She's in the St. Bernardino wing. Near the resident surgeon's office. It's just to your right here."

"Thank you," Paul says and turns to me.

We turn and start to make our way towards the wing. It's still jam-packed with nurses milling around in scrubs, clipboards held next to the chest as they walk by. Two patients are wheeled past the hallway. Gratefully, Paul doesn't make any small talk. Usually, he'd pester me about something or have an idea in his mind that he wanted me to address. I guess the look on Nessa's face has changed everything. He's probably thinking about it.

Though we've seen a lot of dead bodies, dead in ways that are unspeakable and indescribable, we haven't had a case where our one surviving victim is found dead the morning after we'd been in to question her.

The nurse is where she's meant to be. She's sitting on an empty bed in the far corner of the room. The last bed. Near the window.

There's no one else in the room. Good. She's made it so, which I commend her for. I wouldn't have loved it much either if we were meeting outside the room, out in the open and whatnot. We need all the privacy we can get. Paul closes the door behind me silently and then we walk further into the room. The nurse looks up at us with red-rimmed eyes as we approach. She makes to stand, but Paul gestures for her to sit.

"Hi. Ms. Beckinsale," Paul begins, introducing us. I let him do the talking. I always let him do the talking. He's more impressive than me. "We're the detectives from Paddington police station. You spoke to one of our colleagues on the phone, and he told you we were coming?"

"Yes," the nurse says. "He said I should find a quiet place for me to talk to you." She smiles lightly. "This place borders on crazy at times. Not that I'm complaining or anything. So, I found this place for us. I think it's not going to be used in the next few minutes."

"Thank you, Ms. Beckinsale. This will do."

"Call me Jodie."

"Jodie," Paul says, and then asks, "Can we sit?"

She nods fervently. "Of course." We sit. I give Jodie the McDonald's I'd bought for her. She thanks me and takes it but doesn't rip into it right away. She just keeps it on the floor beside her legs. Paul looks at me for the first time since we entered the hospital. He gives me a look that I know means he's trying to tell if I'll allow him to begin the questions first.

Seriously? Is he fucking serious right now? He wants my affirmation now before he speaks. Bloody hell. This guy. I give him a gentle nod. He nods back and then turns to look at Jodie.

He asks, "What can you tell us about last night, Jodie?"

"Like I told the officer I spoke to, there was nothing strange about last night. We had done our checks, and the patients were all in their rooms; it was late, most were sleeping, I guess. I was heading to Mr Hardwick's room; he is on an IV machine, the bag had finished, and I was on my way to change it. The machines make a loud noise when the bag is empty, I wanted to change it as soon as possible, so not to disturb the others."

Paul raises a hand to stop her. "We understand, Jodie. No one faults you for doing your job. I believe there should have been another nurse on at the same time as you?" Jodie nods at this.

"Yeah. Jasmine. But she was running late."

I ask now. "Is she in the building now?"

Jodie shakes her head. "No. She took few days' leave after she learnt what happened to her patient. She couldn't contain the pain." Her voice turns remarkably tense. "She's a very good woman. It's not her fault she was running late; she's never normally late..."

Paul stops her there. "No one is faulting Jasmine either for what happened. Did you hear or see anything or anyone that should not have been around at that time?"

Jodie nods at this and then takes a long breath. Then she says, "No, I was walking past Annette's room and heard voices; they were muffled, but I was able to hear Annette's voice. It seemed she was speaking to someone. I thought she was on the phone as I couldn't hear the other speaker's voice. I wish I had knocked on the door or just popped my head in quickly..."

"It's not your fault, Jodie. It's no one's fault for the matter."

Jodie shakes her head. "I should have opened that door. I could have seen who was in there with her..." The guilt is strong with this one.

"And you could have been hurt or worse," I say. She looks over at me, and her eyes widen a little at the thought of what could have happened. I'm guessing a small part of her is happy she didn't open the door.

A small silence engulfs the room. I sigh heavily. This is going nowhere. We're wasting time. She didn't see anything.

I break the silence by asking her, "Are you sure there is nothing you can tell us about last night?" Jodie shakes her head.

That's a no. She has nothing. What's her use to us? I wonder what she'd told Mark that made him call us so early in the morning. Paul looks at me. I stare back at him in a questioning way. Did I do something wrong? He turns to Jodie and says, "Thank you for your time, Jodie. Thank you again for telling us what you know."

Is he serious? She didn't tell us anything. Nada. I try not to roll my eyes. He stands now. Making me and Jodie join him. He stretches out his hand, and Jodie shakes it.

She nods at this. And I almost tug Paul's coat to pull him out of the room. I force myself to thank her, and then we see ourselves out of the room. Jodie does not come out with us. I guess she still needs some time alone. I wonder what is going on in her head.

Instead, I say to Paul, "So, a dead end."

Paul sighs heavily. "It's not a dead end. Don't say that."

"But she didn't tell us anything. What else do you want me to say about that?"

Paul sighs again. We are still in the hallway, making our way to the lifts to head to the main entrance. He says, "No, she didn't. But at least we learnt something...?"

Looking quizzically at him, I ask, "And what is that?"

"Our killer could quite possibly be someone that works in the hospital," he announces.

"And you sussed this out how?"

Paul shakes his head. "They were able to make it into the hospital, into the ward unrecognised. Probably used one of the hospital's scrubs, a lab coat or a cleaner's uniform and was able to enter Annette's room unseen."

"Nice deduction, Sherlock. I'm guessing you're going to present your theory at this briefing we have."

"I'm going to bring it up. It's basically all we've got."

Paul stops at the front desk again. The nurse, Nessa, is still busy reading the documents in front of her. She looks up at us as Paul leans in. "How about the other nurse? What's her name? Lynn? You were with her last night, right?"

Is he seriously asking about the lady who had been ready to drag him down to the staff changing room and have her way with him last night? At this time?

Nessa seems shocked at the line of questioning too. "Lynn will not be back here till this evening. Would you like me to have her call you?"

"That would be helpful, thank you." He takes out one of his cards and hands it over.

"You suspect the Lynn girl now?" I ask as we walk away.

Paul just shrugs.

Next, we're in the elevator, and I finger the ground floor button. We stand in silence as the car plummets down, and in five seconds, we are downstairs and making our way back to the car park.

We head to our cars. "I'll meet you back at the station," I say.

"Yeah, I've got to make a quick stop, but I'll be right in…" he says as he opens his door and gets in the seat.

"What do you mean you have to make a quick stop? Where are you going?" I ask.

"Don't worry, I'll be literally right behind you… 20mins tops."

He can't be serious. "Twenty minutes isn't right behind, you know that, right?"

He's already shut the door and backing out of the parking space.

I guess I'll see him at the station then.

Chapter Eleven

BRIEFING

Nicole

There are more than a dozen officers inside the briefing room. Almost everyone in the station is present. The room is rectangle with alabaster walls that is boarded up with thick blur panes made of glasses. A brown oak wooden table sits at the centre filled with files and documents. A large panel LCD flat screen is positioned on the far wall to the right of the room. Currently, it is on, but there are no visuals showing on the screen. Several officers mill about the room while others chat with each other; hushed voices, laughs and taps on the shoulder emanate from the room.

I walk in and head to my desk, which I can't actually see much of since it's covered in files. I take my jacket off, put it on the back of my chair, and sit down. I can busy myself with emails before this meeting starts… Have about 10 minutes to kill.

Those 10 minutes fly by, and I realise the meeting is about to start, so I get up and start heading over. Paul comes speed-walking towards the briefing room.

"Right behind you, yeah," I say as he walks up to me.

"I said 20 mins…"

"Where did you go?"

Before he can answer me, our boss, Superintendent Micheal Pangborn, beckons us to come to him. "Anything from the hospital?" Paul and I shake our heads.

"Only thing we came up with is that the perp either works at the hospital or was able to disguise themselves so that they could move freely without being noticed."

Micheal nods. "That sounds plausible. We could consider that."

I want to add something, but before I can say anything, Pangborn turns to the other officers in the room and drums his left meaty palm on the desk twice. The noise reduces abruptly. And everyone turns to him.

Pangborn addresses the room, "You all know why we're here, so let's not beat around the bush, shall we. We've got a shit show on our hands, guys. It's not something we see every day, trust me."

I try not to roll my eyes on this. The dramatics. What does he mean? We for sure have seen similar. The only difference is that those were gang-related and not random people.

He continues after looking at everyone in the room for a moment. "But before we delve into the details and why we are here, I'd like to introduce Dr George Stansted. He used to work with the National Crime Agency – NCA. He's retired now. But he does consultation works and freelance profiling from time to time."

I look to my right to see a pudgy man with red hair and a thick goatee in a double-breasted suit and striped tie ambling towards us. Paul is beaming as he approaches. Dr George barely glances at us when he reaches Pangborn, and then the two men are shaking hands, and our boss gives him the floor to speak. I don't understand what he is going to add. We don't need a long history lesson about serial killers, their styles and whatnot. We need to get out there and do the hard stuff. Not listen to people talk. I want to say this. But I hold myself. Pangborn wants this meeting, and once he sets his mind to something, there's no stopping him. In fact, no one does anything without his say-so.

Dr George greets the room once. Just to get everyone's attention. And then he says, "I've been given a quick run-through of what you have here. I've yet to read a concise version though. But that's not an issue."

Like it was ever an issue. He continues, "I gather that it's still been sorted through, but from what I was able to read, I believe we have a killer that has a fetish, or should I say an abnormal or irrational fixation."

A fetish. Is that all you can think of, Mister Doctor. An irrational fixation? You're just explaining what a fetish is. Where did you get this guy, Pangborn?

Dr George picks the remote off the desk, turns to the plasma screen behind him and presses a button. The screen flicks to an image of a man. Some of the officers in the room gasp as they look at the screen, which shows a man standing leaning on railings but has been propped up somehow. In some ways, the picture seems normal, someone posing, having their photo taken. However, when you look closer, you can see that the eyes of the young man have been removed.

Dr George continues. "The killer takes the eyes of his victims. Seems a little bit illogical at first. But then when we see the next victim and the others, we start to see a pattern."

One of the officers raises his right hand and asks, "Why the eyes?"

"He uses them as trophies. Or his souvenirs."

Souvenirs? Did he just say souvenirs? What a fucking idiot. Souvenirs are not something as disgusting as bloody eyeballs. I firm my palms and feel my nails start to bite into my flesh, and I instantly release them. I glance at Paul, and I'm glad his whole attention is on Dr George. If he'd seen me like this, I wouldn't stop hearing about it. It's like he watches my every move like a hawk. I'm trying to learn how to control my emotions when I'm around him. I take solace in Dr George's not-so-captivating brief.

He continues with, "From what I've learnt so far, or studied so far, the killer doesn't have a particular demographic he looks at.

Most serial killers either go for one or the other sex when choosing their victims, not both. The staging of the bodies isn't in easy places to access quickly. I believe we are either looking for a male suspect or possibly a couple working together. However, the latter isn't a norm for this kind of crime."

I clear my throat here loudly. I can't help myself. "What makes you think a woman isn't capable of doing this?" Several heads turn to stare at me, including Paul. But I pay them no heed.

Dr George turns to me, and I say, "Male and female serial killers choose their victims and commit their crimes in different ways. Researchers have found that male serial killers tend to "hunt" their victims, who are often strangers to them. Females tend to "gather" their victims, targeting people they already know, often for financial gain."

Dr George waves my opinion away as he says, "Can't be a woman. I've reviewed the photos and the autopsy reports. It's definitely a man. Has all the characteristics of a male suspect."

"But you're making any assumption…"

"I prefer to call it an educated analysis." He's giving me this how dare you question me look. Paul lightly kicks me with his foot to get me to stop.

"Your analysis ever wrong?" You could have heard a mouse fart with how quiet it got.

"Not in 25 years. It's a fact. Also, I hate to even have to go there, but it would take a lot of strength to move the bodies around. The victim found by Hyde Park and the other found in Paddington rec would have had to have been brought there, and without sounding sexist, women are just not capable of moving weight that heavy."

"So, women are weak…? Is what are you saying?"

"No, not all. I am, however, saying that there is no way it's a woman, and having seen the victims, I stand on the fact that the killer is a man. Only a man can inflict that kind of pain on victims."

I sigh. I'm in a room filled with patriarchs, misogynists who think women are fickle and can't amount to the same dangerous acts as men. I'm not saying this to be proud of women who commit these types of crimes, just that we shouldn't put anything past anyone; everyone is capable of anything. I see other female officers nodding to his assertions. Idiots. Some of us are the reason we are still where we are.

Dr George smacks his lips and says, "Anyway, I've assumed that the killer favours people because of their eyes."

Paul raises his hands at this and says, "Care to explain more on this."

"I'm about to get to it." This earns snickers from around the room. Paul looks at Pangborn, who has his eyes glued to the screen. I roll my eyes.

"If you look closely at the victims' eyes," Dr George says, swiping to another image on the screen. It shows the first victim, a Black male in his thirties who has yet to be identified as he had no ID on him, Annette and then the latest vic, who has been identified as Joshua Randal, 25, white male. He continues with, "There is something about these victims' eyes that the killer likes. They have been removed with such care that there is little to no damage around the orbital socket; someone would only take that much care about something they treasure. Also, as there was no damage, we have to suspect that the killer has a background in the medical field. Normally, the removal of an eye takes between one to two hours, and that's just for one to be removed; both would be double that. The perp is clearly proficient at what they do, as they were able to remove Miss Smith's in-between the nurses' room checks, which during the night is every hour. The questions that we need to answer is, what is driving him to commit these crimes, and is there any type of pattern that could help us stop him. Looking at the photos of the victims, there is nothing special or unique about the colouring of the eyes. The first male had brown eyes; Annette's were blue, and Joshua's were green. Nothing special about any of them, to us anyway, but the perp clearly likes something about them. He is also able to get hold of some form of paralytic drug, the lab is running a tox screen to find out which one, but this basically means that all of the vics were awake and aware of what was happening..."

"Sick fuck," comes from somewhere in the room.

"I would agree with you. These people didn't deserve to go through what they have. We need to make sure that we stop this guy before he has a chance to do it to anyone else. We should talk to the first and third vic's family and friends, check if either of them reported being attacked recently. I understand that the female had been attacked at her home, and Jay seems to have bruising around his neck, but they looked old and could be from anything. We don't know right now."

Someone from the room mutters loudly, "Is it safe to say that everyone with somewhat nice-looking eyes in the area is in danger?"

Dr George purses his lips at this. He takes a moment to think about this and says, "Not everyone per se. The ones that are unlucky, you might say. Those that the killer somehow managed to get to." I sigh loudly at this.

Paul turns and stares at me. I ignore him. This guy is just lousy. It's just assumptions to him. Nothing more. This is what I've been trying to say. We are in the early stages of this investigation, not all the areas have been covered, and here a former NCA agent and now self-proclaimed freelance profiler is trying to build a case out of nothing.

Paul tugs at my right bicep. I pinch his left palm. He hisses in pain. This draws the attention of Pangborn, and we stop at once.

Dr George is saying, "Now, there is going to be a lot we are going to uncover along the way, but if we do, and I'm able to analyse it, then I'll be able to give you guys a full picture." He nods at Pangborn and says, "The floor is yours," and steps aside from the plasma screen.

Pangborn steps in front of us all and clears his throat. "This is shaping into a very big case. One that we've never encountered.

Not only is our killer unknown, but he is also likely to strike again." He turns and stares directly at Paul and me. "We've got a call from Kensington Met. They've found another body. It sounds like our boy's handiwork."

He turns to the rest of the room. "There is no extra information I am going to divulge here. We don't have much. But we are going to do our best and use what we have. Hopefully, this doesn't escalate more than it already has." He looks at every officer in the room and asks, "Any questions?"

None came. And in the next second, everyone is breaking out of the room. I watch the former NCA profiler walk out of the room. I briefly wonder what he's going to bring to the case. Pangborn points at us and signals we should follow him.

We are walking down the hallway as he addresses us. "The body is now in the morgue. I need you two to go and see if you can get anything we can use to catch this killer."

"Where was he found?" Paul asks.

"On a chair in another park." He shakes his head in disgust. "Bloody fucker left him in the open again like the first one. This one was found by a group of mums taking their kids out."

I ask, "Any witness?"

Pangborn shakes his head. "Galloway had none. Said he and his men made sure to get all the statements from the joggers, runners, and other residents out there. But I think you should try to visit the area before heading to the morgue. Perhaps you can get something that Galloway and his men missed."

He leaves us with this and enters his office. Paul looks at me and nods to the door, and we start moving.

Chapter Twelve

NO WITNESSES

Paul

Nicole left her car behind and hitched a ride with me. I don't mind. I get to look at her more. As usual, she's deep in her thoughts. This time, I don't bother asking her questions that will distract her. I have my own inner conflict to worry about. Some of which is about this case and where we are headed now.

I've been thinking about the body found in Kensington. The fact that the killer went so fast with the next killing amazed me. This proves that whoever he is, he has all the confidence in the world that makes him work as fast as he does. No one has ever seen him. No one has ever heard of him.

I do think Dr George might be on to something. With his deduction and my own, I think we have the killer down pat. There is something about his victims' eyes that he finds attractive. The images on the screen flicker before my eyes now. I see people who are dead just because some weirdo liked their eye colour. The question now is what makes a potential victim an actual victim.

This city has close to 9,745,000 people and increasing. There is no way to be able to protect any of them. All we can do now is just pick the crumbs, whatever he leaves us and pray that he makes a mistake that will help us catch him.

"A penny for your thoughts." It's Nicole's voice.

I shake myself from my reverie and turn to her. "I'm just thinking about the case."

"Really?"

I just stare at her. "What do you mean "really?"

"You know." She shrugs and says, "Whenever I have that kind of forlorn look on my face, you call me out on it. And you won't believe whatever I've got to say about it. So, I just think . . ." She doesn't finish the statement, but I know what she wants to say.

I shake my head. "Are you still angry about the hospital?"

She just stares out of her window. "I'm not."

"But I think you are."

She turns and looks at me pointedly. "I'm not."

I laugh at this. "You're angry again. I get it. I can be quite pestering."

She doesn't respond.

"I'm just looking out for you," I say. "As partners, we are meant to know if the other is okay. You seem lost in your thoughts, most times. I think there is something you're going through that you don't want me to know."

Again, she does not respond.

"Is it your uncle or Marissa? Anyone?"

Silence again. She just keeps staring out of her window.

I sigh and say, "You don't like to share. I get it. But I want to know I've got your back when the time comes. That's all." I watch her bite her lips. And I press the statement home with a question. "Do you have my back?"

Nicole turns and looks me in the eye. She sighs and says, "I've got your back. You don't have to worry about me." She sounds honest, and I believe her. Why wouldn't I? We've been partners for five years now. I'm just trying to know if she is alright with the case.

She says, "So, the case. What were you thinking about?"

I shrug and don't answer.

She punches my bicep lightly and says, "Come on, tell me what you've been thinking."

"I don't think you're going to like it."

"Try me," she says.

"I think Dr George's assessment of the killer is spot on."

Nicole nods at this and says, "Do you?"

"Yes, of course, we know what the killer wants. What his potential victims look like."

Nicole frowns at me. "We don't have jack... The perp has attacked both men and women, they all seem to be in the same age range, and the only thing that links them is that they have their eyes removed. It doesn't take a rocket scientist to work out that that's the only connection. The fact that their eyes are removed is nothing more than trophies being collected."

She makes sense, again. But I don't want to give her this one, so I say, "But you can't deny the fact that this in some way helps us understand how the killer behaves."

"How?" Nicole asks.

"He only seems to have attacked people between their late 20s and 30s." Not the best answer; in fact, the only answer I have. "I just think that we're still too early in the investigation to start drawing these conclusions. We need to really study the victims to better understand what is happening."

"But we don't have that kind of time. The more we try to do this by the book, the more the killer kills more people," I add.

Before Nicole can respond, I spin the wheel to the right, pull through the narrow path leading to the park and stop the car under a row of thin oak trees. It's still 11:20-something in the morning, but the whole place is jammed with people. Dog walkers, runners, mothers walking their babies, and others sitting on benches under the shed, eyes glued on their smartphones. Finding a witness here is going to be a miracle.

Nicole turns to me suddenly. "Why don't we just forget this place and instead head to the morgue?"

"You heard the boss man. We've got to see if someone saw anything."

"But we can't find anyone here. Look around. I know without a doubt that most of these people didn't see anything; anyone around at the time would have had their statements taken. We can see those with contact details and either call or visit later."

"We have to try."

"We'll be wasting our time." I just stare at her. She's serious about this. But we still have to do this. "You can go and check, but I'm staying right here," she says.

"Are you serious right now?"

She nods. "Like a red hot iron."

"You really mean it?" I say, rhetorically because I can clearly see that she meant it.

"Fine," I say, opening my door and dropping my right leg on the floor, "I'll do this by myself then." She doesn't respond. Standing outside, I say, "I'll only need 10 minutes."

She just nods at me. I turn and begin walking the park. I pass several people. A man brushes the head of his ten-year-old son in affection as they trudge past me. A mother sings her baby to sleep, rocking back and forth her pram. Joggers rush by. A ponytailed teenage girl in a denim jacket and mini-skirt with a headphone hums a song and stands across the path, apparently waiting for someone. Pangborn didn't give us the precise location of where the killer dropped the body, which leaves me just using my head to get to find the place, a bench in the park... that's helpful; this park is bloody huge and probably has a hundred benches.

I hate to admit it, but Nicole could be right. We're still fresh into it and just grasping at straws, but due to the rate of the deaths from the killer, I think I agree with Pangborn that we don't have enough time to do this by the book.

We have to move as fast as the killer in order to catch him before he kills again.

I reach what I believe is the correct bench, has to be with the flowers and candles that are lit around it; thank God that didn't take long. There's an old woman sitting on the bench on the opposite side. She's reading a book. Her half-moon glasses pulled a little bit down over her nose. I sit next to her and scan the area. Right now, I'm wondering how I'll be able to get someone who was here that day when the body was found. According to Pangborn, Galloway and his men had questioned almost everyone who was present. I won't be getting something different by coming here. But all the same, I have to try.

The old woman suddenly turns to me. She pulls down her glasses and stares at me intently. "You are with the police?"

I smile at this and say, "How can you tell?"

She gives me a smug smile of her own. "I've been sitting here since morning. No one who has passed has decided to sit here; they just come to look or put things down. I guess everyone feels sorry for someone who passes so horribly. You don't have anything to put down, and you weren't scared to walk up to it." She motions to the other bench.

"I may be innocently looking for someone."

"Oh, don't try to kid an old kidder, dear. You've got the eyes of a police officer. My husband, Jon, bless his soul, was once an officer. He had the same eyes. Especially if he is on the hunt for something."

I don't know what to say to this, so I just keep looking at her.

She smiles warmly now as she asks, "So, I gather the police had been here the other day to question people around when the body was found. No one saw anything."

I nod at this. "That's what I've been told."

She cocks her head to the side and asks, "Then what are you looking for here, dear? What do you intend to find?"

I take a long breath and look across the area again. "Actually, I have no idea. I guess I wanted to see if there was some way I would be able to meet someone who saw something or perhaps see if I can get something by just being here."

The old woman nods and reflects on this for a while. Then she says, "Well, I don't know a lot about you, young man, but I must say your instinct to come here may be right."

At first, I don't understand what she means by this. So, I just say, "Pardon?"

She sighs. "I thought you'd be smarter than this."

I stutter at her comment. Then just stare at her.

"I meant you're in luck by being here."

"You mean . . ." My eyes grow wild. I can hardly believe my luck.

She completes the statement for me. "I was here that morning. And yes, I saw what happened, although I was a bit far from here." She points to a chair almost 25 yards away from us. "And no, I didn't talk to the police. I was going through my monthly colonoscopy test the day they came." She waves a wrinkled hand in front of me. "Don't ask me why I didn't go to the police station. I thought what I saw wasn't clear, and besides who'd believe what an old woman saw while reading in the park."

"I believe you, ma'am," I hear myself say. I can't contain the excitement racing through me now. What were the chances?

She stares at me for a moment and then chuckles. "You remind me so much of Jon. Oh, I really miss him." I don't respond to this, but I give her some time to reflect on it. After a moment, she says, "Every day, early in the morning, I come out here to read. I majored in literature in my university days, graduated to become a lecturer at Cambridge for a while before retiring. I love books. I've been devoted to them since I was a young girl. So, that morning, I settled on my chair and pulled out Thomas Hardy's *Tess of the d'Urbervilles*. I have read the book several times. But each time I open it, it feels anew. There was I on the first page when I saw two figures walk by this way. One was younger than the other. I didn't make out the gender of either, but I know one was helping or should I say dragging the other. At first, I thought it was two people who had a bit too much to drink, one worse than the other, and they were just stopping to get themselves together before carrying on. It didn't look odd to me. But then . . ."

"But then what?" I ask.

"But then I heard someone scream a few hours later. It was the most horrific sound I've ever heard." I can only imagine. And the commotion that came after that. "Later, through the gossip seeping into the park that afternoon, I learnt that a man was found dead on the same bench I saw the two going to. At first, I didn't want to believe it, but my brain told me otherwise."

She looks at me. "I'm sorry, I didn't see them clearly to be able to help much more."

"You have nothing to be sorry for, ma'am."

"No. I should have told the police, should have told someone about what I saw."

"Like you said, you didn't see them."

She stares at me and says, "You're a kind man, Officer . . ."

"Adams," I offer, I'm not going to bother correcting a title.

"Well, Officer Adams, sorry I don't have anything else for you." We're silent for a while, both looking at the people strolling around the park.

Looking at my watch, which reads 11:34am, I stand and say, "Anyway, I'll leave you now so that you can go back to your book."

The old woman waves the statement off. "Oh, I'm not really enjoying the book. It's a thriller of some sort. I don't like thrillers. I'm a literature kind of person."

I stare at her and smile. "Thank you, ma'am. Enjoy the rest of your day."

She nods at this. "Have a good day."

I start to walk away, but she calls my name, and when I turn, she says, "Tell me you're going to catch the person who did this."

I say, "It's our job, ma'am—"

"Call me Theresa," she corrects.

"Theresa," I say.

63

She nods at this statement. Then she says, "Godspeed, then, Officer Adams." I nod once at her and turn and head back to the car.

Godspeed, I think. That is just what we need now for this case. Moving as fast as the killer, and maybe, just maybe, he might slip up somewhere. I know he will soon. I've been an investigator for almost 15 years and there is one thing that is a constant. The perpetrators always slip. And when they do, we'll always be there to catch them.

That said, Nicole was right. We're still fresh to this. We won't want to jump to conclusions fast and miss the most glaring fact. We have to move quickly but at the same time know when to keep a keen eye on everything.

I reach the car and see Nicole on her phone. When I open the door, I glimpse Candy Crush Saga on the screen before she turns it off. I settle on the seat and close the door. She looks at me for a moment and asks, "Anything?"

I shake my head. "Nothing. You were right. There is no one here that saw anything."

"You're lying."

"What?"

She stares me down. "I know you're keeping something from me. I know when you do that. I can see it. And you're doing it now."

I sigh. "If I'm holding out on something, then that means it's unimportant, okay."

She nods and laughs at this. "You're still angry I didn't come with you. So typical."

I start the car and put it into reverse. "I don't know what you're talking about."

"Of course you do. I didn't come with you, and you're still angry about it. That's what you do."

I sigh again. "Okay. Fine. I'm angry. Why didn't you come with me? And how did you think I found something."

While she tries to answer, I'm pulling the car to the road, shifting the gear to first gear and starting off down the road.

She says, "Alright. I'm sorry. I didn't see the need to visit an area that has already been covered. But I see now I'm wrong. I'm sorry."

I didn't respond to this. Nudging my arm and smiling, she asks, "Can you at least tell me what you found there?"

I heave a long breath out of my nostrils. I'm still mad at her, but I tell myself we're still partners, and we need to always be truthful with each other in order to solve this case, so I tell her about the old woman I met in the park.

Chapter Thirteen

THE MORGUE

Nicole

It's almost 12 when we make it to the morgue. I watch Paul pull the car into the parking lot, beside the building. There's next to no one outside but through my window I can see several cars, including a BMW, Volkswagen, and Mercedes-Benzes on the lot. Dealing with death must pay better than I thought. Paul turns the ignition off and steps out, I mirror his movement, and we close the door together.

"Dr Eaglesbert, right?" I ask as we make our way into the building. Paul nods. He'd made the call on the way here, right after he'd finished telling me that story about an old woman he met at the park. On our way here, we realised that we didn't actually know who to meet at the morgue. A quick call to Pangborn who in turn spoke to Galloway told us where to go. And he also told us the name of the mortician.

The building's interior is as empty as the outside. The entrance hall is barely sporting any human presence. It's as if everyone has been sequestered inside their office. Fortunately, we see a plump woman on the reception desk with a name tag NIKKI, fiddling with a file. We walk to her. Paul takes charge as usual.

"Excuse me, ma'am. We're here to see Dr Eaglesbert. Do you mind pointing us to the direction of his office."

The woman's eyes brighten at the doctor's name. "I'll do you one better. I'll call him. He's been waiting for you." She picks up her telephone, punches a number on the screen and puts it on her ear. "Yes, doctor, they are here," she says, and waits for a second. Then, "Okay, I'll tell them that." She places the phone down and looks at us, saying, "Dr Eaglesbert will join you shortly."

We didn't wait long. Almost five seconds after she tells us, man with silver hair and thick goatee in a white coat over a pressed black suit appears in front of us. He's good-looking but in a bookish kind of way. And like all morticians, I don't think this fella has ever smiled since he got this job. However, he manages to appear deferential as he ambles close to us.

He stretches out a hand to Paul, "You guys must be the detectives from Paddington. It's nice to know that you could make it." I groan internally at this. It isn't by any means nice. We're just disturbing him, and out of some courtesy, and because he'd been pressured to, he's accepting us. I'm sure he told the lot at Kensington the same thing he's going to tell us, they could have told us themselves, they just didn't want to deal with the lower riffraff. I can't believe even the police are boujee about areas.

Paul shakes his hand and says, "Correct."

Dr Eaglesbert turns to me with an outstretched palm too. I shake it and start off, "I believe you told Kensington how the victim died, even submitted a report. We may be encroaching here since we can go and collect your report from Galloway, but we'd appreciate it if you give us another rundown of the report."

Dr Eaglesbert waves the statement away. "It's not a problem. I'm glad I get to tell it to someone else. The victim's cause of death is, or should I say, are rather interesting. Not in the good kind of way. Don't get me wrong. Whoever that did this to him is as inhumane as the Nazi doctors in Auschwitz."

Paul and I don't comment on this.

Clearing his throat, Dr Eaglesbert says, "If you can follow me, please. I'll take you to the body."

We follow him down a hallway. The light from the bulbs is faint, casting low light on the creamy coloured walls. The sound of our footwear on the tile floor echoes as if we are inside a snare drum. I don't see anyone here. This makes me want to think that it's probably only Dr Eaglesbert that frequents this part of the building. Perhaps his assistant isn't here, I think, but he may not have one. He cuts to his left, into another passage, this one with no light at all, just one window to our right that a brief ray of light from the outside of the building streams in. As we approach some of the doors, I feel goose bumps forming on my skin. I don't need to be told that behind those doors were refrigerators used to store corpses.

The mortician pushes open a door to his right and enters. The chilliness of the room hits me as I walk in with Paul. I like cold, but not this kind. I particularly like winters. Damn, the cold always has that calming effect, but this is a morgue. The morgue looks exactly like every goddamn morgue I've ever seen in my life. A long stainless-steel table, an LED flashlight, and long shelves lining the walls around the rooms. Dr Eaglesbert beckons us to follow him. He arrives in front of one of the shelves and pulls one out. The body is covered in a faded blanket. Dr Eaglesbert shifts the cloth down to the victim's chest.

The victim looks like he's sleeping and could wake at any moment, however we know he won't. There is dried blood around the sockets, but other than that, nothing. The victim seems to remain at ease, like he's been induced from the pain, which is saying something because this is how the other victims are. According to the toxicology reports, what was found in systems were traces of etorphine. It's a strong analgesic used to sedate animals. A full dose can practically be used to bring down an elephant. It's strictly governed by law.

Dr Eaglesbert says, "I would guess that your victim was alive while the killer was removing his eyes. The etorphine was to keep him still; he would have been awake and could feel everything but would not have been able to move or make a sound."

Paul asks, "You said that the etorphine was for him to get the victim's eyes out?"

Dr Eaglesbert nods.

"What about getting the victim to the park?" Paul asks.

"I think he gave him another dose mixed with a small amount of adrenalin to keep him going for a while, which would have stopped him from going into shock," Dr Eaglesbert said.

I ask, "How did the victim die?"

"From an overdose, I think." Dr Eaglesbert heaves a long breath and then says, "I managed to get some bits of information from Galloway. About the case you're investigating. You've had other victims such as this. All of them are killed the same way, I understand."

We both nod, and I take step around the body. "What we know so far is that the killer restrains the victims with etorphine and then proceeds to remove their eyes; we have no idea how long they are kept for. One of the victims was attacked the day before and then killed in the hospital, the others have been left in public places all posed, like some form of statue That is all we know now."

Dr Eaglesbert nods at this.

Paul says, "We wanted to see if there is any difference with this victim."

"I'm afraid not," the mortician says. "It's the same thing here. The autopsy report shows etorphine in his blood, several doses, which resulted in his death. He isn't injured anywhere, cancelling any assumption of any other assault."

I ask, "Did you get any DNA prints?"

He shakes his head. "No, ma'am. He was wiped clean."

Paul adds, "Or he was wearing gloves all the time."

Dr Eaglesbert nods and says, "It's what I thought too. It's possible."

I sigh inwardly. This is just what we've got from the previous murder. A victim dosed with analgesics, and his or her eyes removed. No prints on the victim. Blood reports show an enormous amount of etorphine in their blood. There is nothing to work with here other than the fact that the victims seem to be helpless when the killer starts to inflict pain on them because of the sedative. There is no print left on them to help narrow a string of searches for the killer.

Paul says, "What I don't understand is how he managed to lead the victim to the park even in his delirious state. Two full doses of the analgesic would surely make the victim immobile."

This was about his conversation with the old woman. No doubt.

Dr Eaglesbert considers this for a moment and then says, "He may have waited until they were on the chair before administering the second dose. He wanted the victim's last day to be on that chair in the park."

Paul does not respond to this, he just continues to stare at the victim's corpse, lost in his own thoughts.

Dr Eaglesbert looks at him and then at me. I assume we've overstayed our welcome, the poor mortician must have something else to do. I nudge Paul to wake him from his reverie. He startles a little and then turns to me.

I say to Eaglesbert, "Thank you, we'll see ourselves out." The mortician nods and starts pushing the body back to the shelves.

We walk out of the room, and once we are in the hallway alone, I say, "Where did you go?"

"What?"

"Back there, it seems like you were lost in your thoughts."

"Oh, I was thinking about the case."

"Oh, yeah?"

"Yeah. I was wondering if we're even going to catch this guy."

"We will," I say.

Paul ignores me. "I mean, he's so meticulous. He's way ahead of us and has all the time in the world to commit as many murders as he wants."

"He's going to slip up," I say, "one way or the other. And when he does. We're going to catch him."

Paul looks at the empty floor in front of us and says, "So, we're back to square one."

"Yeah."

"We have to wait for the next murder scene to see if we can make any headway in this."

I look at him and make to say something, but I hold myself.

"What?" he asks.

"Never mind," I say, shaking my head.

We return to the entrance hall and see Nikki reading a paperback novel. We walk past her, and she doesn't look up from her book.

Chapter Fourteen

CHRISTMAS IN MAY

Killer

Rainy season can be a bitch at times. I'm donning a parka over a fleece jacket, over a wool-knit cardigan, high-high boots with thick, double-threaded socks and still the chill from rain seems to penetrate into my skin. I don't like walking in the rain. Times like this I stay indoors. But this twat has chosen this day and time to walk in the open.

The fuck is he doing now? Yeah, like I'd thought. Talking with a friend. Christ, man! It's raining like hell out here and you want to stop and chat to everyone you see. It's like he knows everyone in the area. Right. I forgot he lives around the corner. But who stops in the middle of a rainstorm to talk to someone?

Oh, he's done talking. He's now moving. Alright. Lead the way. The weasel is outfitted in a red parka. His pantsuit is soaking wet. He looks like a little kid in that outfit. Red parka, pressed suit that's at least one size too big for him; what an idiot. I've met a lot of nerds in my life, believe me, but this guy beats them all. Any other time he would have been looked over, however his eyes got me. They are green but with brown around just from the centre like a firework. I just have to have them.

I see him turn to the road to his left. He stretches out a hand, flipping it up and down to slow the car coming to his right. I look in time to see a Ford race into view. Its headlights blurry from the rain. The weasel runs into the road and is able to get to the other sidewalk before the car can reach him. I wait for a moment, not wanting to make my presence known to my target, and also, I don't want to get crushed by any car speeding on the road. People don't what to be held up in the rain,

They're all in a race to get home, or to their various destinations, so they will certainly not see any pedestrians due to the haze. I wait a moment so that am sure the road is clear. When it is, I rush in and fall in step again. There is little foot traffic here, so it doesn't take me a moment to spot him again. I see him 30 yards away from me. He's not particularly in a hurry. Just a normal man heading home after work. Except that a normal man would be in a mad-dash to get in out the rain.

We're basically the only two people at ease strolling under the rain. I don't mind. His destination is my destination. So far, when he arrives, I'll be behind him. I don't get the time to survey who he is or where he lives and works. I was just outside, walking with a few commuters when I saw him. He seemed lonely. Well, all of them are lonely. He was sitting by himself, fiddling with his coffee. He held a phone in his left hand, which I assume he'd just taken a call with. I think it was bad. Perhaps the wife or fiancée had called to break things up, he didn't look like he was taking it so well. He'd kept his face forlorn, a far-off thought running in his mind, and his Harry Potter glasses askew over his nose.

It was then I saw his eyes. I thought this kind was mostly seen in women, but here is one that seems to break that notion. The man, just like the rest of them, seems to have given up his home in the world. I'd been on my way home, but I stopped, and after staring at him for a while, I decided to follow him. I don't have my usual equipment, but that doesn't matter. I don't engage them on the first meeting. That is a rule. I've learnt not to rush into things until I understand fully what I'm getting into. It has saved me a lot of times. And I haven't slipped.

He's stopped in front of a building. It's among a row of buildings that stretch further down the street. It's a four-storey affair. Painted in a faded white colour, it's boarded by shuttered windows. I stop 25 yards away from him, making sure I'm as inconspicuous as I can be. He looks up as if contemplating if he should go in or not. The fuck? Dude, is this your house or not? He stands almost a full minute before heading in. I watch him turn to his right and begin climbing the stairs that lead to the front door. I wait a second for him to progress further up the stairs, and looking up and down the street, I follow.

It's a respite to get out of the rain. I shake myself on the stairs to remove the water on me. I scan the place, seeing just a dim room with closed doors. I don't give it a second glance and start climbing the stairs. I no longer hear him, and I'm forced to pick up my pace, but then just eight stairs above me, I hear his footsteps. It's slow but steady. Jesus Christ. Has this guy ever moved fast in his damn life? I slow my pace when I'm five stairs behind him. I don't want to spook him. The less he knows someone is behind him, the better.

He makes it to the final floor, the building's last floor. And as usual, I give him time to progress. I come out of the darkened stairwell and fall in step behind him. I watch him scan the doors as he walks—is he checking to know if the other tenants are at home, or is he waiting for someone to open the door for him? This makes me wonder if this is really his place. I'm about to turn around and move back to the stairs when he stops in front of a door.

He's going to see me through his peripheral vision, so I turn to a door beside me. He wriggles a bunch of keys out of his pocket and scans it. The LED light above us is clear but a little bit dim; he manages to fish out the key and insert it into the door. I see him glance a moment in my direction, checking me out. As if he'd seen me here before. I'm holding a bunch of keys out, too; none of them can open the doors around here. But I act like they can.

He stares at me for a while and then heads into his flat.

I snatch the keys back to my pocket and move out of the door. So, this is you... Now I know where to get you. I'm not overly bothered if he's seen my face; it won't matter. My mind starts feeling giddy at the thought of getting all my toys together. I put on a small smile as I spin around, head back down the hallway to the stairs, and start making my way down.

Just then, my phone pings. My other phone. I wonder who it is, but still fish it out of my pocket as I walk. I'm perplexed at first when I see the eyes and green leaves emoji on the screen. I don't remember who I saved that number with. I chuckle to myself. At the irony. It's not like most of them remember me. But then I remember the woman with her wandering son. Carla? Yeah. That's her name. I was wondering if she was going to call.

Nah. Scratch that. I knew she was going to call. Maybe not now, but later. I've met women who are so bored with their lives that they won't miss the chance of making fast friends with strangers they meet for the first time. Trust me. She looks like she isn't getting much attention from her husband. Or she is a single parent. I've met this one too. Seeing Carla for the first time, seeing her eyes were nothing special. However, the way she spoke to her son is what put her on the chopping block.

Executing what I do efficiently in the most secure city in the country is not easy. There are bound to be ups and downs. There are days I don't make it work, and there are days I do. All that matters is perseverance and skill. I've worked mine to be top-notch. I stalk the city day and night without fear; this is all achievable because I'm just that damn good at what I do.

Chuckling to myself, I answer the phone. "Yes. Who is this?"

"Hey, hi ... It's Carla. Carla James, we met the other day at the park. You brought my son to me."

Of course, I remember. "Aww, yeah, I remember now. How is he? Hasn't ran off again looking for centipedes, has he?"

"Haha, he's fine, thanks, no he hasn't." Carla giggles at this and then pauses for a second,

"I was wondering if you were free any point this week? We could get that coffee. I could show you around the area a bit and introduce you to people."

This is like Christmas in May. I've never had any of them invite me over so willingly. I'd have to drop a few hints or use my powers of persuasion. Some see me as a very attractive person, and so the rest is not that hard. But a mother with a son and her cutting the time to invite me out is not what you see every day.

I say, "That is so generous of you. Thank you. I would love to."

"Good," she says with finality, as if that is what she wanted to hear. I fight not to roll my eyes. She has no idea what she's inviting to her home.

"Do you remember where we are?"

Yes, I say to myself. "No, other than you're on the other side of the park, near the station, I think."

"Close. We're a little further up from the station, I'll text you the address. You can meet us at the house, and we can walk up to the café."

"Sounds like a plan, I've got to run, but I'll look out for your text and let you know when I'm free, okay." Don't want to sound so happy about her calling.

"Sure, sure. I'll let you go. I'll text you, okay, bye."

"Bye."

I'm back outside in the rain now, walking back the way I came, in a much better mood than what I was 20 minutes ago, I have a few things to start planning. Mister man would have been fun. However, I think Carla is going to be more fun. To be fair, I know where he is. I'll come back another time and get those peepers.

Chapter Fifteen

INSOMNIA AT THREE THIRTY

Paul

I toss and turn over my sleek sheets. I can't get any sleep. It's as if my whole body wants me to remain awake. Against protocol, I'd drunk two glasses of Merlot, and yet instead of feeling light-headed and dizzy, I feel like I'm on speed.

I rise and sit on the bed. It's a four-poster affair. One of the things I loved about my ex. Caroline always wanted the best. If not that, then just forget about it. I try not to think too much about her or remember the reason why we separated. It was very messy. No one was at fault. But as usual, I took the blame. Yet, it didn't change a thing.

I look up to see the time on my alarm clock, and it is just three thirty. I'm supposed to be up and ready by five, but I guess sleep is far away from me tonight.

Sighing heavily, I rub my left palm over my face and yawn. The case. It keeps flickering through my mind. Like disparate elements that need to be arranged. Only these elements don't even make sense to begin with. We know the killer's signature. He stalks them and then attacks them at first; later, he comes back to finish them off. So far, it has been established that he somehow disguises himself so much so that no one recognises him.

After visiting the morgue, we'd returned to the station, where a stressed Pangborn told us that the CSI team from Kensington were going to submit their reports to our team even though they didn't want to, not that it's going to matter anyway, they have zero leads and nothing that could really help. We've all established that the killer is so meticulous he'd not leave any prints. The case was getting murkier and started to feel unsolvable. We'd talked a while about our findings in the morgue, which was not so different from what the Kensington police had, and there wasn't any input anyone could give at this point other than to continue going over the reports, photos of the victims and crime scene and any statements that were taken.

All we can do is wait for the killer to strike again and hope that he messes up somehow.

But I don't want to wait. The lives lost are enough. Waiting is as good as just watching the killer murder someone and not doing anything. It's more like inaction. I don't want that. There must be something we have here that we're missing. I've raked my head, going over everything, hoping that I remember seeing something that we may have missed, anything that is certainly out of the ordinary. All that comes to mind is just what we have so far. My afternoon was spent going over everything, but nothing.

After so many hours of thinking and analysing, finishing almost half a bottle of wine, I tell myself that I need some sleep. I've learnt early in life that a well-rested brain is the best tool for leaping over a hindrance, and I have a couple. So, I showered and headed to bed. But a second in, I don't fall asleep. It rained this evening, and I got soaked, I hate the rain. It's cooled the air and, in turn, made my bedroom cool. Which would have normally been superb sleeping temperature; however, sleep seems to be far away from me. My doctor will call this insomnia, but I don't see him these days, so I'll stick to the fact that I'm just restless.

I realise it's the case. I'm still thinking about it.

I won't be getting any sleep for the rest of the night. No doubt. Better to make good use of the time. If the case is making me restless, then it is better I address the situation. Since I became a detective, partnering with Nicole, I always prided myself for the meticulous way I analyse and solve cases. Nicole is the same. This made me love the fact that we are working together.

But recently, she seems to be pulling away.

I sigh.

Nicole would be asleep now. Every other sane human would be asleep now. But not me. I sigh again. Let's get on with it. I slide out of bed and trudge to my wine shelf near my kitchen. The bottle of Merlot is still half empty, but I finish it by pouring it into my glass. I take a deep gulp and cringe as the liquid races down to my stomach. Ahh. That is definitely going to keep me awake. I turn and make my way to my study, holding the wine. Switching on the light, I blink a few times to adjust my vision.

On the rear wall is a whiteboard. Dotted with photos of victims and etched with markers and drawings correlating all of them to an unknown. The unknown is the killer. There have been four deaths so far, including the man left in the park. I made sure to include what we know so far.

The disguise. The fascination with eyes, the use of etorphine to sedate his victims, the fact that the eyes are removed with surgeon-like precision and that he wipes them all down, leaving no trace evidence, no fingerprints, nothing.

I'd started this a day after the first murder happened. I guess that was when the insomnia started. There haven't been any recent additions, but that is just saying. I'm sure this night, with my restlessness from this case, I may be able to make something out of the few precious hours before morning. I sip my wine and study the board again. Everything seems accounted for, and yet, there is something in my mind that keeps telling me there is more than what meets the eye.

I don't know if it was from the old lady. Theresa, is it? She said she saw two people walking in the park. One was helping the other, not that they were fighting or that one was trying to get away from the other, which had made her not give them a second glance.

How can someone's frame be disguised like that? So it's not possible to make out anything about them.

Was he overdressed? Certainly, that morning might have been chilly. But if so, Theresa must have noted it. Old people are very attentive, even when we think they're on their way to senility. And considering the fact she's a woman, she won't miss any detail for her life. Then why didn't she see the other person? I think the figure she saw was moving in another form. Certainly, the killer wanted to look as inconspicuous as he could, but even at that, Theresa should be able to discern what sex they were.

I mean, she easily identified the vic.

I fix my eyes on the 'UNSUB' I'd written at the centre of all the victims. I'd circled it just to emphasise how detrimental it is to us that we don't know who it is. Theresa, not being able to discern the figure helping the vic in the park, activates a series of thoughts in my mind – each of them blurring out the rest. And now it is flashing through my head as I stare at the board.

Let's say, for shits and giggles, the killer is a woman?

Yes. Nicole could be right. I won't tell her this, though. Or else it's going to get in her head. I mean, she corrected Dr George at the station, and everyone just looked at her like she was crazy. They, including me, were all certain that the killer was a man. There is no explaining someone who removes the eyes of his victim, most especially women, to be anything other than a sadistic man. Just like the good Dr said, men are more brutal. I mean, not trying to sound misogynistic, but all the characteristics are pointing to a male figure.

But now I am having second thoughts, and everyone should.

Theresa couldn't place the figure because he'd changed how he looked. I'm thinking a man in his late forties helping a man in his mid-thirties in a delirious state like that after taking the analgesic would appear suspicious to anyone around the park that early in the morning. But a woman would not raise an eyebrow. She could be his wife, his sister, his daughter, or even a friend just helping the man that day.

Now, this could be just my mind playing tricks, but trust me, I've checked all angles.

Nicole must have seen it, too, considering she suggested it. But if this is the truth, then it changes everything for us. For the whole of the investigation. We're looking for a female killer and not a male. This could also explain why the female victim seemed well at home when they received her. And it could also explain the use of the etorphine sedative. I know I can't just explain everything with facts, but I know that I have hit the jackpot. Not in the proverbial sense.

God, it feels good to see some developments for once.

I stare at the board for a moment and pat my trousers for my phone. Only to realise that I'm in my boxers. My phone is in my bedroom. I sip my wine again and turn to the door, walking back the way I came. I need to call Nicole. It's best she hears this now and not tomorrow. I assume she'll be working on the case in her home too.

I step into my bedroom, eye the phone on the bedside table, and pick it up. I pull up Nicole's number and call her. And the call goes to voicemail. What the hell? She always answers my calls. I momentarily think that she's probably visiting her family (when she usually does this, she turns her phone off), but there is no way she would, not now, not with this case. I try her number again, and it still goes to voicemail.

Bloody hell.

What now? I look at my wine and then finish it in a single gulp. Well, insomnia at three thirty in the morning isn't a bad thing after all. I might have just made a breakthrough, one I couldn't do in the afternoon with Nicole. I guess this is it. I stare at my alarm, which shows it is five to four. I could still try to salvage some sleep before it's morning. Lord knows I need some, even if it's a little. I feel like today is going to be a very long day.

Chapter Sixteen

LIKE A FLICKER HERE THEN GONE

Colin Hargreaves

What the heck? What is happening to me? A sprinkle of light blurs my vision. A rustling sound emanates in front of me. I try to blink my eyes, but they feel like lead. The hell. That sound again. Like a flicker here and then gone. It's hushed but strong. Is someone talking to me? I try to move, but I can't feel my body. It's as if I'm made of lead. What is happening to me? The rustle. The lights again. And then the hushed sound. I want to scream at the top of my lungs, but it feels like my voice is gone.

The lights come again, and darkness covers the blur. What is... it shifts again. Then comes into view. The rustling sound follows. I assume that the darkness is someone. Whoever it is, is the one that is making the sound. The light could be a bulb overhead or a handheld torch. The son of a bitch that put me in this state is hovering above me, and I'm pretty sure they're the one trying to talk to me. *What the fuck do you want from me?* I yell, but it is all in my mind because I can't move my lips.

I'm still squirming or think I'm doing it. Nothing is real to me at this point. The thought of how I got here flashed through my mind. The last thing I remember is I was about to open my door and felt something sharp piece the back of my neck. I'd groaned and tried to rub at it, thinking it was an insect... that's it. I can't remember anything else.

What the hell have I been given? I can't move; sedatives don't make you immobile – I've been doused with that a lot of times in my not-so-young life. When I was small, I suffered a traumatic accident. Broke my hip. The pain from the injury lingered even after I'd healed. My doctor made sure I received the necessary sedatives and also made sure that I didn't become addicted to them.

But not this. Whatever my captor has put in my system is way more than a sedative. If Mathias was here, he'd be reading the goddamn medical rules and regulations for illegal drugs. He would tell me the name of this drug, I'm certain. Oh God! I want to shout. Make it stop! Whatever you want, I will give it to you. But nothing comes out. I'm not making any sound, but I can still hear the voice of my captor. It is faint, but I can hear them...

I take through my mind the people who would possibly want to do me harm. I'm not that wealthy. Not Bill Gates or Elon Musk kind of wealthy. But I have family wealth. The Hargreaves have basically been the sole owners of the finest leathers in the country, well, until those damn Italians came. My parents didn't participate in the day-to-day activities of the company. My father wanted to distance himself from it as far as he could, and my mother supported his every decision. But we still received some small portions of the company's profit, courtesy of my grandmother's will. She always loved my dad. Some of my relatives said my father was her favourite child. That should make the other siblings envious of him, I think.

That said, I know several people who'd want to do me harm. First would be Danil Stefano, my associate partner at Massey & Coopers. I know that he's been eyeing me ever since my boss, Janice Melchior, promoted me to VP. He was really eyeing that job and should have gotten it had he not messed up and been caught spending the company's money on exotic dancers.

And last but not least are my cousins from my uncles and aunts – the ones that I have never spoken to since I turned 18. The ones that want nothing to do with me but want everything to do with me because, in some way, I am part of my grandfather's will. The news came as a shock when my father died (my mother had passed away when I was just finishing high school), and their family lawyer came to my apartment one evening and read the will to me. I have been bequeathed to handle one of the Hargreaves's department stores in Regent St. According to the lawyer, it was one of the biggest stores. I'd wondered how this came to be, but the lawyer had calmly and patiently told me that it was all the workings of my grandmother. Right before she died, she forced her husband to put her estranged son's son in the will. And that he did. Before she died, she'd managed to make me a millionaire a thousand times over. A woman I haven't met in my life.

The will is still being finalised, but you see why my cousins from my father's side would want me dead. You see why these people would want me dead. But if they actually paid someone to get me, to put me in this very state, then why not show their faces? It's been a long time since I've seen them, but I've dealt with enough rich people to know that they don't miss the chance to gloat at what they are able to do. Rich assholes that will be better off from this world. Oh, I'm among them now. I guess, in some way.

My vision suddenly clears a little now, but my eyes feel really dry. I blink, but my eyes feel like sandpaper is being dragged across them... There you are!! Who the hell are you!? Why are you doing this to me!? I know they are talking; I can't work out what they're saying, though; everything sounds like I'm under water. What the hell did you give me!? Still nothing, What the fuck are you smiling at, you asshole? Was that a fucking flash? What the hell you taking a picture for?! Why are you showing me a scalpel? Oh Jesus! A sudden tremor rocks my body. Next a needle appears. I see the crystal vial inside the syringe, and then it disappears.

I feel a prick on my arm. It's the only feeling I'd gotten since I became conscious. That dick's just injected me. The scalpel returns. The fuck. It disappears, and a scissor appears. This disappears, too, and they show me two other items, but I have no idea what they are, and I honestly don't care what they're called. I just don't want them used on me.

They've just dropped something into my eyes, which I should be grateful for as it has helped ease the scratching feeling. I can see over to my left, and there's an assortment of what I can only assume is medical equipment. They're moving closer, with something from the table that looks like kitchen tongs just smaller... In my eye? What are you doing? I can't blink... Oh God, I know who you are? I read about you in the paper. Why me? Please, please don't do this... Dear God, please don't let this face be the last thing I ever see.

Chapter Seventeen

SOMETIMES, I JUST CAN'T HELP IT

Killer

Sometimes, I just can't help it. Of course, there is my visit to Carla coming up in a few hours. But you can't expect me to just keep still and wait until that time. I need to satisfy my urge. Yeah, sorry. I forgot to mention. It's like an urge. I can't just keep still and wait for the predestined time to reach. No. Hell, no. I need an outlet. And what better way to do that than to find another person.

Don't get me wrong. I'm a patient person. In fact, I'm the most patient person in this world. But sometimes there is a time when the most patient snap. And this is me. Here. Now. It's been two fucking days since I dropped Jay in the park. The appearance of a body in a completely different area miles away from the last one they found is no doubt baffling the police. This, of course, was always the plan; they will never be able to work out any sort of 'hunting ground'. My hunting ground is all 607 square miles of this lovely city. They'll dedicate so much of their precious time trying to make heads and tails of everything, I could probably keep them busy for the next 10 years if I wanted to.

I have a series of potential victims around the city. I've been staking them out. In a city with over 9 million people, I am a kid in a candy store. People in this city are so wrapped up in their own lives that some have never even spoken to their neighbour that they have lived next to for years. All you have to do is take your nose out of your phone and take in the sights around you, and you'd open a whole new world that most don't see.

This guy right here is Colin Hargreaves. I came across him while I was out jogging. He hadn't been paying attention and bumped into a homeless man on the street. He started shouting at the man to watch where he was going and that he was lucky that he hadn't spilt his tea on his suit. Which, in fairness, did look nice. He looked at me as I jogged past as if daring me to say something to him, and there they were. The brightest brown eyes. They looked like melted chocolate. I, of course, needed to have them. I had continued down the road a little, then crossed over and followed him from the other side of the street. His face looked familiar, but I couldn't place where from. When he stopped and turned down a side alley, I crossed over and acted as if I was stretching and watched him enter a door. Checking to make sure there was no one around, I went to the door and on a little gold plaque in black writing read Hargreaves leather. I turned back and headed back out the alley and crossed over the road. There was a bus stop further up, so I went and sat and pulled out my phone.

A quick google search brought up all the latest news about Hargreaves leather. Been around over 60 years, blah, blah, blah, takes in over a million a year. Damn, owned by Thomas and Mary Hargreaves, was passed to their grandchild after they died... okay a lot of history... there's a picture, BINGO. Hello, Colin Hargreaves.

According to the website, Colin became a multimillionaire overnight. The Hargreaves are among the richest people in the whole of the UK. Old money that seems to have spread to the grandchildren, who in turn will be able to stretch it out to generations to come even if they decide to begin squandering it.

But I'm not looking for money. Nah. Not at all. This isn't about the money. It's been two days since I was last here. Luckily for me, Colin is just getting back from work. You can leave work when you like when you own the company. He looks stressed, I wonder what happened today. Stressed, however, for me is a good thing because stressed means not focused, which means your guard is down.

Colin is in that state when I get him. He just opens his door (I'd been following him, and he was so lost in his own world that he didn't hear my footsteps). I hit him in the head with a rock from the front garden – make sure you don't leave stuff like that lying around – before injecting him with a little tranquilliser, enough to knock him out but to keep him on his feet. I go into his home and lock the door.

Thank God, the man is alone. It would have been a bit complicated had he not been, nothing I wouldn't be able to handle, though.

I carry/drag him through the place, trying to find the perfect spot. We get to the living room, and I see that he has a balcony that overlooks the building's back communal garden by the looks of it. I plop him down on the sofa and stand at the glass doors. This really is a lovely place. There are several pathways leading around the garden and decking area that's furnished with tables and rattan garden sets; there's even an outdoor kitchen with a gas BBQ. His balcony has a little two-seater set with a coffee table facing the garden, which is a perfect setup to leave him. For now, though, let's close these curtains so that no nosy neighbour can look in and see us.

Time to set up. I give Colin a full dose of etorphine because I know by now the tranquilliser will be wearing off. He jerks awake, and for a moment, I think I should give him another tranquilliser, but then he slumps back and starts to sleep again. Next, I started removing everything I need – scalpel, needle, speculum, scissors – and place them on the table. Fuck. Fuck. Fuck. I gave him a full dosage when I should have given him half of it.

Shit. Shit. Shit. I'm going to have to wait for him to wake up or give him a shot of adrenaline to wake him up. Which I do. It lasts close to four or five hours. I didn't check. I am too desperate to look at my watch. When he wakes, I let him get conscious enough before I start talking to him. I realise he isn't hearing me when I speak, but I still continue. This is just normal procedure for me. I give him a run-through of how I met him, how he became an interest for me, and then proceed to ask him if he remembers me. This looks like pure madness, I know. But in the few days I've been watching Colin, I'd appeared in front of him once.

I'm wondering if he remembers. I repeat this act with all my victims. But none of them know who I am. I wear a disguise, I know. I'm not memorable, I know. But, like I said, this is just procedure for me. Finally, I start showing him my equipment, and this triggers a series of shocks throughout his system. He's under the influence of a drug that should keep an elephant at bay, but yet here he keeps rocking back and forth like he's on speed. Hastily, I retrieve another syringe and jab it into his arm. It's half the dose but still deathly. He'll certainly die, but I don't care.

I'm almost done with him.

As I watch him go under, I pick up my scalpel and reach towards his face. Now, this part is the hardest. Not to me. I've been doing this for a while, and I am way past the disgust. But to anyone, gouging out an eye is one of the nastiest things to do. You'll be incising into the soft ball, past the cornea, past the tendrils of vein, and then the bone. Using the scalpel and scissors makes the experience much faster. I'm able to make fast work of the right eye. Blood spurts on my medical gloves as I work, but I don't mind. I soon move on to the left eye, and I make fast work of this too.

I put the two eyeballs in a medical bag that goes into my backpack. I stare at my handiwork for a little. Colin's face is now a mask. Blood from his hollow eye sockets drips down his face. Sometimes, I take a moment to reflect on what their life would be like if they didn't have such wonderful eyes. For Colin, he'd probably handle his share of the inheritance expertly. He seems like an upright guy, even though his girlfriend left him. Not his fault. Pulling off the medical gloves from my hands and jamming them into the bag, I snatch my bag and walk out of the house.

When I'm outside, I begin to think how long it will take before the police find the body. They should get the call from Colin's workmates or relatives. When he doesn't respond, someone will come and find him on his back porch. Then the police will arrive. I wonder if the detectives after me will think of this. I've made sure to remove any form of prints relating to me. I've wiped them clean. A smug smile appears on my face. Nothing beats being ahead of the game.

Heads and tails again, I think heads and tails.

I look at my watch once I'm in the street. It is still a few minutes before morning. I have a lot to do before I meet with Carla. No pressure. Hew. This is going to work out exactly as I planned. Come Monday, those babies are mine.

Chapter Eighteen

NO LUCK ON ALL SIDES

Nicole

"I called you in the morning," Paul says to me as he picks me up from my house.

"Yeah?"

He nods. "Yes. And you didn't answer."

I shrug at this. "Must have been asleep. I'm sorry."

"But I don't take you as a deep sleeper. I mean, you always wake up whenever I call you."

Where is this coming from? "Well, I was very weak and tired for the first time. I had to rest. I went into a deep sleep. Is that an issue?"

Paul stares forward into the windshield for a moment, then says, "It's not. It's just that I wanted to talk to you about something. About the case, to be specific."

I nod. "What about the case. Do you know who the killer is?"

Paul shakes his head. "No. Not that. I just discovered something."

I fix my eyes on him. He continues with, "First of all, I want to say you're right."

I'm right? That is a first. Paul admitting that I was right about something. Most times we have to argue things out, even when he knows full well that I am right. It's like arguing with two sides of a Mobius script. "How am I right?"

"The killer. You suggested in the brief that it could be a woman."

I just nod.

"Well, you're right. It's a woman."

I ask, "How do you know?"

Paul quickly explains his thoughts on what the old woman had seen in the park. Why wasn't she able to figure out who the second person was, the one helping the vic? He says that this was possible because the killer was disguised in male clothing that must have hidden her face. If she'd been closer, her profile would have been clear, but that far away, anyone could mistake her for something else.

I internalise this for a moment. It feels right. At least it can explain why Theresa, the old woman, couldn't see the killer from that distance. I mean, if I was wearing a man's clothes and someone saw me that far away, I'd be unrecognisable.

I say, "Good thinking, Paul. How did you think of this?"

Paul starts the car and pulls it into the road. "Don't ask. I had some sort of insomnia yesterday; well, it has been happening ever since we started this case. Went to my drawing board and just stood there thinking."

I smile a little at this and say, "See who is nocturnal. Later, you'll say I'm the strange one."

He laughs at this. It is a hearty laugh. "Don't start."

"Why? You don't miss a chance to make fun of me whenever you can," I say.

"Well, now I know how it feels. And it is no longer funny."

I ask, "So, what are we doing today?"

"Mark called this morning. Said that a body has been found in Rock Creek. Has all the markings of our killer."

"Bloody hell, which is so fast."

"Exactly what I thought too. It's as if she's not waiting. She knows we can't catch her."

I did not respond to this.

Paul continues, "Well, Creek police have secured the area, and all we have to do is just scan the place." By this, he means we need to see how the murder happened. The body must have been moved, so all we will be dealing with is just the empty death floor.

"What's the name of the vic?"

"Colin Hargreaves Windsor."

I blink at this. "You mean the. . ."

Paul nods. "Yeah. The one and only. He's the great-grandson."

I don't know the name Hargreaves, but I do know Windsor. They're one of the most successful families in the country. All from what the Americans call old money. From making leather. After the Italians, they have been the next best thing. Paul gives me his phone, and I see a picture of a man in his mid-forties. He has one of the clearest blue eyes I've ever seen. Now I know why the killer went for him.

He says, "Mark sent that over. Since we won't make it in time to see the body, we will be working with this."

"Anything to know about him?" I ask.

"Not much. Father distanced himself from the family, hence taking the name Hargreaves. But, according to the family's lawyer, it seems that the father's mother loved him so much he forced the husband to include his son in the will. The father didn't know about this, of course. His mother never tried to tell him. But when all had died, including Colin's father, the lawyer came with the great-grandson Colin and told him about his share in the family's wealth. That he was the owner of the largest department store in the country on Regent Street."

"A beautiful future cut short," I mutter under my breath.

"Yeah," Paul agrees. "And the bitch isn't even looking for money."

What? "What?"

"I mean, the killer, she obviously didn't kill him because of his wealth."

I tap his phone screen and say, "He's got one of those eyes, dude."

Paul nods. "I know."

I let a small silence engulf us as I spy the Rock Creek signboard in front of us. Paul expertly manoeuvres the car through the little traffic and turns the wheel into a zero-lot neighbourhood lined with trees. Rows of two-storey buildings roll down on both sides of the street. There is little to no foot traffic outside. It's like one of those streets that celebrities and business magnates live in.

"What did you say Colin did again?" I ask.

"I never said," Paul replies, but then adds, "He's an accountant at Massey & Coopers."

I scan the street as I say, "Didn't figure an accountant would stay here."

"Well, seems like he makes good use of his pay check," Paul replies. We find Colin's house packed with police cruisers. Several of them were milling in and out of the building. Some nosy neighbours are already out on the sidewalk and gawking at the police activities. For a neighbourhood this silent, this incident must have been a kicker. Paul pulls further down the road and stops the car. We come out of the car, lock the doors, and cross the street.

A uniformed officer raises his hands to stop, but we both flash our badges, and Paul says, "Paddington DCIs. We've been sent here."

"Let them through, Seamus," A voice that belongs to another uniformed officer says in front of us near the stairs.

Officer Seamus waves us through, and we trudge the stairs to meet the other officer. He says, "Right this way, sir and ma'am." He leads us into the building.

As we walk, the officer, with a name tag Moorhead, talks us through what they have done. He says, "The coroner just took the body away. We've done well to sensitise the scene with the help of the CSI unit. They are still at it now."

Paul says, "Have any theory of how the killer came in?"

Moorhead shrugs and says, "He must have surprised the vic at his door. I think he knocked him out. And then things went smoothly here."

Paul and I exchange glances for a while.

Moorhead catches this, and before he can say a thing, Paul just shakes his head and says, "It's nothing. Go on."

Moorhead motions to the door leading to the back porch behind the house with a woodsy backdrop. "He takes Colin to the back porch and starts working on him immediately."

We make it to the porch where a bunch of CSI units dressed in white jumpsuits with medical gear are combing the area. Yellow police tape demarcates them from the rest of the floor. The porch is filled with white oak tables and tabletops and complete with folded umbrellas. It's as if I'm looking at a summer lounge, except for the dried pinkish blood that coats the floor. It is more than messy. The killer had laid Colin on the table while he worked on him. Bits of the veins on the victim's eye sockets were splattered on the chair. I know this isn't from struggle or anything, but the way the killer removed the eyeballs.

Moorhead says, "I don't know what you guys want to find here, but I'm certain there is nothing here."

Paul nods at this. "Yeah. You are right." He turns to the officer with a tight smile on his face. "But that won't make us stop the CSI from doing their job, will it?"

Moorhead laughed. "Nah. I'm just here to secure the scene. They have their job. I have mine."

I move around the table, still giving the blue and white tape a wide berth, eyes scanning the floor. I don't know what I am looking for in particular, but I just want to make sure that I cover all corners.

Moorhead concludes with, "I'll leave you guys now. Good luck." He walks away.

Paul turns to my direction and asks. "Find anything?"

I shake my head. "Nah."

He shrugs at this, but he follows me to start looking at the scene. After a moment, he asks, "Why take him out here?"

I stare at the woods to my right. "I don't know. To have fresh air and a view while they work."

Paul looks at me eerily. "Seriously?"

"What?"

"You really think that the perp wanted a 'view' while they worked?" he says.

I just shake my head. "You wanted my opinion."

He mutters under his breath. "Yeah, but not that."

I don't reply to this.

Paul sighs and says, "We're wasting time here. There's nothing we're going to find."

I rise to my full length and say, "You're right. Another death, and we've got nothing."

Paul nods. "Yeah. But something tells me our killer is getting more comfortable. It's just time before they slip up, and we get them for good."

Before I can respond to this, however, one of the members of the CSI unit turns to us. It's a woman in her early thirties with a shock of red hair in a ponytail. "Excuse me, sir and ma'am, if you could step out of here a bit, we're still working the scene," she says.

I shrug and mutter under my breath, "Not that you'd find anything."

Paul hits my arm with a balled fist. Aww. I rub it with my left arm while he says to the CSI woman, "We're sorry. Please continue." I see the woman looking warily at me from my peripheral vision as Paul drags me out of the room.

Once we're in the living room, Paul says with a seething tone, "When will you learn to work on your interpersonal skills."

"I was just telling her the truth."

"But that shouldn't be the way to do it."

I sigh. "I'm sorry if I was a little bit upfront."

He smiles. "A little bit is a bit of an understatement."

I turn and give him a stare.

He says, "Don't start complaining if I start analysing your behaviour."

Before I can respond, Moorhead appears in front of us with a straight face. "Guess you didn't get anything from the scene."

"Yeah. No luck," Paul says. More like no luck on all sides.

Moorhead nods at this. "Well, we just need to hope that the CSI guys get something."

No luck on that, too, I think.

Paul smiles. "It's all we are asking for now."

"Yeah," Moorhead concurs.

I say, "We'll leave you guys to take care of things."

Moorhead nods, and then we are heading out of the building. Once we are on the porch, Paul says, "Want to head back to the station, or . . ."

"Or what?" I ask.

He shrugs, "Or you'll be going home."

Knows me like the back of his palm.

He stares at me for a moment. "You're going home, aren't you?"

I don't respond, just continue staring forward in the direction of his car.

"Come on, Nicole, you can't just leave me every day, every morning and go home. We are working on something here."

"It's not every day. Don't say that. I'm going to visit my mum today; that's why I'm leaving."

A concerned look creases Paul's face. "Is she alright?"

"Had a few rough days recently, but doing okay," I say. "Thanks for asking."

No one speaks again as we reach his car.

Chapter Nineteen

MAKING NEW FRIENDS

Carla

"Sorry, honey, Mummy is very busy. Can you look for it by yourself?"

Jordan snorts a reply, and the house grows silent again. Whew! I've been hard at work since morning, making preparations. The doorbell is going to go any time soon, and I'm not yet done. It's not like I have something to do. I'm basically a stay-at-home mum these days after Proctor and Smith fired me for missing a board meeting seven months ago. Yes, it was an important meeting; however, it was the same day I walked in on my ex-husband Neil with one of his colleagues going at it in our home office.

To be honest, looking back on it, I'm happy for the break. The break from them and from him.

Ten years and the only person I have left after what he did is Jordan. Who I'm so thankful for.

These days, I just stay at home and take care of my six-year-old son. Other times, I walk to the library or the park. Go for a run, I've taken up painting at one of the local colleges during the day, and I'm getting pretty good at it.

All my so-called friends deserted me as if I was the one who was caught cheating on their significant other. It's as if they were never there. I'm not overly bothered, as it showed me who they all truly were. However, it has left an adultless void. Other than my father, who lives up north, and a few childhood friends that live out of London too. It's only me and my little man.

Working P & S did afford me one thing. Being their top advertiser for the last 20 years did pay a good salary, which has allowed me to take some time off and not work, and Jordan's father has all but blocked both of us on all platforms. The last time he spoke to Jordan, he said, "I'll come see you next weekend, champ," ... that was seven months ago.

The people in this area are nice, I guess. They keep their distance after the whole cheating fiasco. The men don't want to be seen as being too friendly with the newly single neighbour. The women are polite; they smile, wave, ask how Jordan is, and invite him to outings with their children. Which is nice of them to not leave him out. I hear the chatter of dinner parties and game nights that happened and get told: "It was so last minute, it was only a few of us, or we didn't actually plan anything, but one thing turned into another. We'll call you next time."

Who would have thought that a chance encounter in the park, because of Jordan running off, would lead to a possible potential friend?

Jordan walks in with his hair wet. He's just came out of the bathroom. "Mummy, are we still going to the park today?"

I smile at this. He's been looking forward to this day.

"Yes, hun. Go bring a towel so I can dry your hair before we go."

He nods and runs off to the bathroom.

When he comes back, he stands in front of me while I tussle his hair with the towel. In the mirror, I can see him eyeing the muffins on the table. Normally he would have to have lunch before his treat. However, as we'll be out over lunch, I guess he can have something now.

"Do you want to have one now before we head out?"

His smile almost reaches his ears. "Yes, please."

"Okay, help yourself, pick one and go sit in your chair. Don't touch all of them, just the one you want."

He nods and runs over to the table, picks a big chocolate chip muffin and sits in his chair.

I need to run and change my clothes before we go out.

I rush into my room and quickly slip out of my house clothes. I have a quick shower and do my hair.

It's just a walk around the block, nothing to overly dress for. Why is it so difficult to choose something to wear? I've had a lot of clothes pulled out of my wardrobe and laid on the bed. What to choose. Sighing, I pick a cream-coloured top, light blue jeans and a pair of plain white Nike trainers. Looking at the mirror, I work on my hair and put it into a tight bun. I do a little make-up, not much, don't want to look like I'm overly trying. I think my face is better without it anyway, and I've had confirmation from people that this is true, but I just apply a little, just to add a little something.

When I make it downstairs, Jordan is eating his second muffin, I shake my head at him. I should have moved them from the table before I went upstairs. "Enjoying it, are we?"

"Ummhmm," he murmurs with a cake-filled mouth. I nod and smile at this. Who wouldn't enjoy a good old homemade muffin? They do look good. I think I might have one, too, before we leave. Just as I make my way to the table, the doorbell chimes.

Turning to Jordan, I say with a smile. "I think our guest is here."

"Yayyy." He beams at me. I head to the door. There is a blurry image in the front door window, the silhouette all in black as the daylight frames it. I open the door and giggle. I guess I missed the memo about wearing all black everything.

"You look like you're about to rob a bank, all black hoodie, black t-shirt, jeans and black boots and backpack. You got your gloves and ski mask inside there?"

"Haha, yeah, some other things too."

Chapter Twenty

HEART OF A DEMON

Paul

As usual, I wake up at six thirty in the morning and rub my eyes to get the cobwebs off. I yawn a little, and I immediately cringe. My breath still smells like a frog went in there and died. I guess this is what you get from not brushing your teeth before going to bed. The stale Merlot still hangs on my tongue; my taste buds feel on fire. I rub my eyes again and try to get the fuzziness off my vision.

Something had awoken me.

I hear the sound again. This, I recognise at once because it's the sound of my phone. I always keep it close to my bed. For a moment, I think it is Nicole that is calling, but when I lean over and snatch it off the table, I see Mark's number. Jesus Christ. Don't tell me we've already had another one. I'm incensed by the very thought of this.

Still, I give a long sigh and answer his call. Mark's voice is, as usual, calm. "I hope I didn't wake you."

"Nah, I was already up. Why did you call? Have they found another body?"

"Yes." His response sends a chill through my body.

"What is it this time?"

"Our guy has stepped his game up. God only knows what's going through his head. If you think he was bad before..."

With my body full-on trembling now with what Mark has said, I ask, "What happened. Who is the victim?"

"It's not 'is' but are. A mother and his son were killed. I just got a call from Sarah at Kensington; she just couldn't stop crying. It's awful. The photos she's sent here. . . I can't get it out of my head."

Oh my God. Mark seems like he is going to cry himself. But I don't let him get to that state because I quickly say to drag his mind back to his duties.

"Send me the location and call Nicole."

"Okay," he says meekly.

I ask, "Have you notified Pangborn."

"No. I was thinking since you're one of the leads in this case, you should get it first before I send it to the chief."

I fight myself not to retort to this. I am technically not the lead in this case. Nicole and I are the same in this case. We are the only leads. Mark should know this because he's been updating us since we began working together, but at times, I think he dislikes Nicole. A lot of people do. I guess it's her nature. I have just learnt to live with it.

But I don't correct Mark on this. Instead, I say, "Alright, send it to him pronto."

"I will, sir." Before I can respond to this, he'd already cut the call.

I sigh to this and scroll to Nicole's number. It's six forty in the morning. I'll be waking her up. I know this, no doubt, but it's better to wake her. I call as I dress and prepare to leave my flat.

She picks up on the first ring. "Hello." Her voice is groggy. Definitely waking up from slumber.

"There's been a new vic, or should I say two vics."

"What?"

"You heard me. A mother and her son down in Kensington. I just got a call from Mark, who received it from Sarah."

"I don't understand. Why two victims? And a kid, for that matter."

"I don't know. Perhaps the kid got in the way or something. We'll know better when we get to the crime scene."

"Okay."

"I'll pick you up. I'm getting ready and will be leaving mine in 20. Be dressed and ready in 40."

She just snorts at this and cuts the call. Well, she's getting pissed. Normally, she'd have said something witty.

I guess today she isn't in the mood.

Tossing my phone on my bed, I yawn again and feel my stomach rumble as I stand and walk to the bathroom. I should get something to eat as we make our way to Kensington, I make a mental note. Fifteen minutes later, I'm all dressed and ready to move. When I move to get my phone, I see a new message from Mark. It said that an unknown woman wants to see me later in the day. An unknown woman? I think as I pocket the phone. Could it be a witness? My mind flashes on eerie images of the victims. What could they want with me? I don't think much on this because I need to get to Kensington with Nicole as quick as possible.

I ignore Mark, grab my phone and keys and head out to my car. I don't send him anything when I pick up Nicole. I don't tell her anything as we drive towards Kensington. But in the back of my mind, I am raking my brain, trying to work out who else would want to see me concerning the case. The only people who know about the case are either others on the case or people in the media who have been reaching out almost every day. However, they would all leave their names and messages, if anything. So, who the hell wants to see me?

I'm still thinking about this when we pull into the street. I used the address that Mark sent to my phone, but I'm surprised when I realise that the crime scene is just beside the park where another victim had been found just a few days ago. I wonder what the chances are. Did the killer see their next victim just as they were in the process of leaving the other vic?

Nicole looks at me, and perhaps it seems she knows what I'm thinking because she says, "What a strange coincidence." Tell me about it.

Like the usual affair, there are several police cars parked in front of the home. It's a street property with houses on either side of it, which has most of their inhabitants out and about their doors, craning to see what has happened. Some are already gossiping to each other with the little they know. The police had strung their blue and white police tape around the front porch to separate the rest of the neighbourhood from the crime scene. We get out of my car and cross the road, and after we make our way through the little crowd in front of the victims' home, we approach one of the uniformed officers close to us.

We show him our badge, and he lets us through. We walk up the stairs and enter the house. There are several officers still milling inside. It seems the CSI unit has not yet arrived because the officers are just talking with each other and keeping a wide berth from everything in the house. I see a dining table filled with all manner of delicacies. I feel my stomach rumble. I forgot to get the bagel from McDonald's when I was going to pick up Nicole. Well, I've convinced myself that it's for the best. According to Mark, this is one of the most disturbing scenes he'd seen, so it's best nothing is in my stomach.

"This way," I hear Nicole say, and I walk towards her.

"It's in the bedrooms."

I stare at her. "How did you know that?"

"Heard one of the officers as I was coming up the stairs."

"I didn't hear anything…"

She says with an edge in her voice, "Well, if you stop and get out of your thoughts, then you can know what is happening around you."

I sigh at this. She's right. I've been so in my head the last few days. We make it past a couple of other officers and down a hallway that has two doors on the left and one on the right. There is a large window at the end of the hallway, where you can see the houses on the other side of the street. We walk a little further down and then arrive at a single open door with several police officers standing in front of it.

A man in a brown sports coat and jeans with dark brown hair notes us approaching, leaves his crew and starts making his way to us. I know who he is before he reaches us. This is Gerald Thompson. He is the lead from Kensington.

He stretches his hand out as we arrive. "Morning... DCI Thompson." I shake his hand without responding. He takes Nicole's hand too. Then he says, "It's good that you guys made it here now. At least, it's better we have the same shared minds in the room."

I ask the only thing that's been on my mind, "Can we see them?" He physically cringes from this. I wonder if it is because of how upfront I was with the question or because of the nature of the scene.

But then he says with a gesture to his right into the bedroom, "Right this way."

I see Nicole give him a cursory look before walking into the room. Yeah, tell me about it. If that is not weird, I wonder what it is. I step into the room right after Nicole and physically feel the chilliness in my heart expand again in my body. It's a large room. Scanty at best but still filled with cupboards and pictures. A four-poster, a little bit larger than mine, sits at the centre of the room. But I don't note the make of the bed now.

All my vision focuses on what is on it.

As my eyes take in the crime scene, I feel my stomach rumble. I haven't eaten anything yet this morning, but I feel like I'm going to be sick. Through my peripheral vision, I see Nicole looking at me with a concerned look. DCI Thompson is saying something, but I can't hear what he is saying. I really want to vomit.

Like. Right. The. Fuck. Now.

Without a second thought, I spin to my right and push open a door. Luckily, it's a bathroom. I dash to the toilet and heave the Merlot and biscuits I ate the night before. As I do this, the image I'd seen just a few seconds ago flashes in my mind. What kind of human would do that? To a child in the first place. Oh my God. What is wrong with this fucking world? I heave watery salivary content into the toilet. Someone with the heart of a demon most definitely. I feel a surge of anger ripple through me. I'd been treating this case as just any case, but no more.

This changes everything.

I heave again, but nothing comes out, and as I rise to my feet, using the back of my right sleeve to wipe the vomit from the sides of my mouth, I make a promise to myself that I am going to see that this killer is caught. Such evil should not take a second breath with innocent people out there. Such a menace needs to be sent to the darkest prison in the city or even shot by firing squad. I am going to see to it that this monster is caught.

I return to the bedroom and find Nicole and Thomson looking at me with concern.

My partner asks, "Are you alright?"

"Yeah. I ate a lot of crap last night mixed with some wine. Not a good combination. Needed to get it out."

Thompson doesn't look convinced. "Are you sure?"

Looking Thompson in the eye, I say, "I'm okay. Now, can we get on with this?"

"I'll leave you two to it," Thompson says, leaving the room, and then he mutters under his breath. "Lord knows I've seen enough."

Chapter Twenty-One

WHO I REALLY AM

????

It's self-deprecating when you have to hide yourself all the time. Hide who you are to the rest of the world. Not that you have any other choice. You know deep down that if your true self is revealed, it doesn't matter what you say or do; no one is going to believe or trust you again. There's no other choice here. You know that who you really are cannot be entertained by anyone.

The real you will be perceived as an abomination if seen by the rest of the world.

They say that snakes shed their skins occasionally, depending on the temperature or habitat. Some say it's kind of a defensive mechanism against predators, others say it's an assault technique to be able to capture prey in the thick forest or water. For me, I will go with the assault mechanism. Some snakes are designed to strike. Check out the rattlesnake or the green mamba; what these creatures have in common is that they can camouflage the colour of their skin in areas that have the same shade of colour as their skin.

Don't fucking mention chameleons.

I detest them. I detest how small and insignificant they are. Almost next to lizards. I compare how I do what I do to how the snakes shed their skin and put on another. The change of colours from chameleons is not that. They just want to hide from their predators. I, on the other hand, just want to be able to get to my prey.

Well, enough said about that. What I'm trying to say is that I've long since built my cover. It is staunch and solid. And the last thing I need is to be discovered. People have been trying over the last few weeks. The people I work with at the station are actually funny to watch, all of them trying to work out who the "menace on the city" is, that quack of an expert who was brought in to "help". What a joke! The best has been Paul. He, for some reason, has taken this case to heart. He's been my partner for close to 10 years now, and I've never seen him like this before. It's funny; we've been on several cases together, cases I've helped solve, mind you, and he has no idea who I really am.

Truth be told, I haven't made it easy for him. We've known each other for years, and the guy hasn't met any of my family. While I, on the other hand, met his last girlfriend. Katie, I think it was? I have also met his other family, or perhaps the ones that are still alive. The guy lost most of his family when he was younger, never said how. That being said, I don't have so many relatives left in my life either.

Only my mother, Susanne, is alive.

They have both asked to meet each other, don't understand why. I managed to put Paul off by telling him she was sick. Cancer or something or the other. That had stopped all the questions about when can we meet, do you two want to come over for dinner, blah blah blah. Truth is, I don't want him to meet my mother. She alone knows the real me, and she might reveal something I don't want Paul to know. So, I need to keep her as far away as I can from Paul. I tell him that I visit my mum some days, and I do, just to check in and keep an eye on her.

However, I haven't seen her that much over the last few months.

Yeah. Shocker. I know. But seriously, I've lived under that woman's shadow enough. As an only child, I've been treated with so many things that I detest to this day. I mean, what are the chances that it won't make me grow up and be the way I am now. When I was younger, my parents had me tested and it turned out that I have an

IQ of 198. A high score and close to or more than what Albert Einstein had. I am extremely intelligent. I aced all my subjects and courses throughout my schooling career.

But those challenges were so below what I craved. I wanted to control. I wanted to be superior. To be able to design things the way I like them. That is why I do what I do. I needed an outlet. Some might call me a psychopath or even a sociopath. I like to think I'm a perfect mix of a little of both. See, a psychopath suffers from a lack of remorse, guilt and empathy. They pretend to have emotions. A sociopath is able to feel emotions, although they might be at a shallow level. A psychopath is manipulative and charming; they are precise and calculated. Sociopaths can be manic in their actions; they are normally unplanned, and they leave lots of evidence behind.

I think clearly, I can charm my way through a crowd of people to get to what I want. There's no mental health reason or some sad, abusive childhood that some psychiatrist could blame. No. I'm none of that mental deficiency nonsense... I do this simply because it's fun, an outlet, a hobby.

Everyone has hobbies – things that they love doing. What I do is my hobby. Some people paint, some read, others play an instrument, some go to yoga, others like to play golf. People do all of these things to relax and unwind. Some people love to go skydiving and bungee jumping because they crave the rush, the thrill that they get... Well, so do I. The thrill of the hunt. I feel like a wild animal tracking its prey, following and stalking till the right moment presents itself, then... STRIKE!

And just like an artist, I put my work on display. There's no point in creating work and being selfish with it.

To be able to carry out what I do as efficiently as I do, there are many things that come into play. First is to have confidence. That has never been a problem for me. Second is to always rely on what you know. Working in law enforcement as one of the lead detectives for the area allows me the grace to know all I need to. I can plant information or evidence or even remove it when I see fit.

Third is to have the ability to carry out what I do quickly while not leaving a lot of damage behind. The removal of one's eye is called an enucleation operation and normally carried out by an ophthalmologist; the operation can take a few hours to carry out, double for both eyes. In my younger years, I studied medicine. I had thousands of medical books. At one point, I did consider going into the medical field; however, I chose not to as it would have been a bit more challenging to carry out my extra-curricular activity.

I don't regret what I do. Like I've said, it's a hobby, an outlet, if you will. I guess I would be called a serial killer. I don't like the term, seems very crass. If I don't do this, I may engage in something more sinister. Oh yes, being a serial killer is goddamn evil. But I don't give a shit. I also don't care that I had to kill Carla and Jordan. Shit happens. Some things are unexplainable. Did they deserve it? They were such a loving family; this I know without a doubt. The answer is no. But I don't care about that. Carla brought that up by being mean to her son and having those eyes. How could I let them go? Aww! It's Jordan I was sorrier for. Poor kid. He was too young to leave this world; all he had to do was stay downstairs.

But I had no other choice. All he had to do was stay downstairs playing with his Lego.

What could I have done? Leave him so that he could potentially report me to the police or kill him and let him die with the secret of who I really am and let him be with his mother. Okay. Enough with those guys. I'm up for the next fish. I don't need to plan for his that much. I see him as someone who would easily be taken. All I have to do is execute it efficiently. That is what I am good at. I'm with the damn police department. With the team that is even investigating my killings.

The irony, right?

But that is just by my making. I joined the force so that I can keep an eye on the rest of the officers. There's no chance of being caught in the act or still planning to do it if I am on the team that is looking into the murders. This way, I can keep an eye on every single activity in the department. Although, recently, my partner is really getting on my nerves. He is going to finally figure things out. This I can feel deep down, and I know that if he finally manages to get to it, I need to be ready to remedy it.

I already have a plan.

The fucking old lady. Ever since he spoke to her, he seems to be narrowing things down quickly. Well, it's not totally the old lady's fault. I shouldn't have said something about the killer. Shouldn't have said it was a woman. It was a ploy to play on the masochistic bastards in the department. Never did I think that it was going to germinate into this. Now Paul believes wholeheartedly that there is a female killer out there. After visiting Carla's house, I'd noted how fixated he was. He was pissed. Everyone in the room was pissed, alright, except me. But his was different. I saw that moment of desperation on his face; someone who is going to stop at nothing until he finds the person who murdered those innocent people.

Well, I'd be ready for that.

Oh, speaking of the devil. He's calling me now. I glance at my phone for a moment, considering if I should pick up the call or not, but I soon change my mind and stretch my right arm to retrieve the phone. Even though I am cautious of him, I still want to know what he knows.

Chapter Twenty-Two

A BLINK OF HOPE

Paul

I cut the call from Nicole. I was calling to let her know that I wouldn't be able to pick her up this morning and she should just make her way to the station. She has her own car, after all.

I send her a text instead.

Text Message

Tuesday 24th May

Hey, I've got an appointment this morning so won't be in till later

Tuesday 24th May

Morning, okay no problem, see you later.

The reason I couldn't pick her up is that I have to meet someone else, the woman who wanted to see me.

It turns out that it was Theresa. As soon as we were done reviewing the body at Kensington and returned to the office, I'd gone to Mark's cubicle and asked to know who the woman that wanted to see me was. When I heard Theresa's name, I smiled. How did that woman know what department I was in?

Mark had said Theresa wanted to see me at her home. He then mentioned that she specifically said that I shouldn't bring my partner with me. I knew Nicole and Theresa had never met, so where the sudden exclusion came from, I didn't understand. Anyway, I heeded to her warnings and did not tell Nicole about it.

When I got home that night, I was wondering why she didn't want to speak to me with Nicole present. There was no reasonable answer to this. All I can think of is that Theresa just wanted to speak to me. That would be ideal, considering we had formed some sort of bond the last time we spoke to each other at the park. But something about it still nagged at me. Why be so adamant that I was to go to her alone?

I was lucky to sleep that night. No insomnia, thank God. I think four glasses of wine would do that. I slept like the dead. When I woke in the morning, the thoughts returned to my mind again. It was there in the shower. There as I got dressed and there when I went to my car and drove to the station. It was fucking there as I texted Nicole. Well, no need worrying about something I don't know. . . Yet.

Let's just see what Theresa has to say.

The GPS on the dashboard guides me to Theresa's home. It's a four-storey affair. Painted in a faded white colour, and it looks a lot different from the other buildings on the rows down the street. The colours of the other houses were just too bright and fresher than her own.

I get out of my car and walk up to her porch. Before I reach the landing, the door opens and a smiling Theresa ambles slowly out of her door. She's wearing a shawl over a printed shirt and an almond-coloured long skirt.

"Hi, again, Mr Adams. Sorry, I didn't inform you that I'd call."

"You don't need to be sorry at all. I'm surprised that you even called," I say with a smile, and then add, "But I'm happy that you did."

"Oh, son. I thought they stopped having these kinds of you once we hit the twenty-first century." I don't know how to answer that, so I don't respond.

Theresa beckons me in, saying, "Sorry for my manners. It's a bad habit to keep a visitor at the door. Come in, come in."

I step into her home, and I take a moment to internalise what I am seeing. Theresa's home may not be a beauty outside, but inside, it was more than beautiful. The walls are painted in a bright rosy red colour, pastel blue, and ambient yellow. The furniture is well arranged inside the four hundred square feet sitting room. A large plasma screen hangs on the far wall. The dining table is just off the centre sitting room, beside a window shrouded in embroidered curtains.

Theresa says, "I know. Most of the people I have over here have the same look once they get into my home."

I look at her and ask, "What look?"

"The this-is-not-what-I-expected look."

I smile. "No. I don't look like that."

"Of course you do," she says in a reassuring tone. I shake my head and turn to scan the rest of the room.

She says, "Anyway, it was my son that did the change. Jon and I wanted to keep it the way it was. We weren't very keen on redecorating and all that. We lived in the jazz times, the hippie period, and so many other things. We've seen a lot of change, and we concluded that it is enough."

"I understand," I say, nodding as I stare at one of the paintings of her and Jon on the wall. They were still young and fresh.

Newly married, I guess. "Not everyone likes change."

Theresa rolls her eyes. "Tell that to my son."

The statement makes me turn to look at her. She smiles and says, "I have three sons and a daughter. None of them thinks that change is strange."

I say, "Perhaps they seem to overlook the importance of what has always been."

"Please, you can make yourself comfortable," she says, gesturing to one of the chairs near me.

When I sit, she asks, "Can I get anything for you? I have cookies, toast, bread, or cake." She smiles. "I'm sorry for the sugar-infused menu, but my granddaughter just had her sixth birthday. So . . ."

"That's nice, I'm guessing she loved being spoiled by Grandma?" I say.

She waves it away. "Oh, it's nothing. To me, I mean, it's what grandparents are for, spoiling their grandchildren."

I nod in understanding. She takes her seat, and we lock eyes together for a while. I say to break the silence. "You called me here for—"

"You know why I called you here. It's something serious, and I need you to listen." The caution and the seriousness in her voice startles me, but I don't want to show it.

I make to speak, but she raises her right hand to stop me. She says, "I know you have a lot of questions, and I promise I'm going to answer them or think I will answer them."

I just stare at her. I desperately wish what she has to say will have a blink of hope in it.

She inhales and says, "What is the name of your partner?"

Well, this is starting off well. "Her name is Nicole Murphy. What's this got to do with her?" I haven't forgotten the fact that she specifically asked that I shouldn't bring my partner here.

Theresa replies with, "It has everything to do with her." She takes a long, deep breath and says, "Do you remember when I told you that

I didn't recognise the figure that was walking with the gentleman who was found in the park?"

I sigh, knowing where this was going. I say, "I already figured it out. It was a woman. Wasn't it?"

Theresa is physically shocked by this, and it shows in her face. But she says, "Yes. How did you—?"

"Call it a hunch."

Theresa gives a small smile but remains looking sombre. "You really remind me of Jon." I stare at her, waiting for her to continue, which she does as she says, "I think I saw her face."

Looking into her eyes, I ask, "Who did you see, Theresa?"

She does not reply but just continues to look at me.

I ask again, "Who did you see?"

"Do you really want to know?" she asks.

I sigh again. Woman, I'm trying to give you an audience here. I sigh again and say, "Yes. I want to know."

She looks grimly at me and says, "It was your partner. Detective Murphy."

Oh! Shit! It can't be, though; Nicole is a decorated police detective who has been working for years and has helped close multiple cases.

I say, "Ah, um, Theresa, Detective Murphy has been working in the police force for years. She has helped catch people like the killer we're trying to catch."

She looks at me like she'd heard that her food is about to burn. Then, she says, "Then, my boy, I would say that you have a very dangerous individual working with you." There is a deafening silence, and the room suddenly feels smaller and like there is no air.

I stare at her for a while. Her eyes burn with nothing but the truth. I see an old woman who is a hundred percent sure of what she is saying. I sigh because I know that I truly don't want to ask her, but I don't have a choice.

"Are you sure?" I ask. The tie around my neck starts to feel like it's being tightened.

She looks grimly at me, nods and says, "Without a doubt, it was her. She was the one I saw. I couldn't place her face well then, but when I saw you two arrive at that house a few roads over. I knew that I had seen her somewhere. Then it all came back to me; I had seen her at the park, and as she was coming out of that woman's house."

I just stare at her. Words drying from my mouth. What. The. Fuck?

Chapter Twenty-Three

AN UNBELIEVABLE TRUTH

Paul

I stomp on my gas as I speed away from Kensington. The words of Theresa still echo in my mind. It was your partner. She was the one I saw. I'd argued with her if she was right about this. And she'd said yes,. I couldn't believe my ears.

The analytical part of my mind believes what she says, but again I think I need to talk to Nicole first about this, hear her own side of the story, and see what she has to say about this. But deep down, I know that she won't come clean for me. In our normal conversations, she's not always that open to me. I've always had a feeling that she was hiding something from me.

Was this it? Why her mind was always elsewhere whenever we talked? And there are other instances where it seemed like she knew more than she was letting on.

When I'd left Theresa, I promised her I would be careful while I conducted my investigation into what she had informed me. She was already agitated at the fact that I would still have to be around Nicole while I worked. I promised her that I would take care. While I was stepping down from her porch, I went to pull my phone out of my pocket to call Nicole and ask to meet up, but I stopped myself. Telling her that I have a witness and possible suspect could set her off and could either result in her hurting someone else or doing a runner. I needed to meet her face to face.

How could she do these things? The sight of that woman and her son flash in my mind. A child? What would make her to do these things? Let alone to a child.

When I reach my car, I decide that I need to see her now. Thankfully, due to the fact she doesn't like driving when we're working, I often either pick her up or drop her home. Imagine, if she is living this double life, she's arrogant enough to have a fellow detective know where she lives. Granted, I've never been in her place, now that I think of it. Whenever I've gone, she's either outside already, or I call when I pull up.

It just can't be her; maybe she's got herself into some sort of trouble with someone, and they have been blackmailing her to cover up their mess. Who better to clean up a crime scene than someone who would know what the police would be looking for? And this is why no evidence is left behind... but if it is her doing this, of course she would not leave anything behind as she already knows what we would be looking for? Maybe the real killer has her mum and is threatening to hurt her unless she does these things. Could this be why I've never met the woman? No, Nicole is smart. If this was the case, she would have dealt with it or let me or Pangborn know so we could help her. I need to find something that might tie her to this case.

As much as I want to find and talk to her. I know I can't just accuse her of something, just from the word of a little old lady. I've been doing this job long enough to know that you need to bring hardcore facts to back up your suspicions, not circumstantial evidence.

What am I doing? What am I doing? This is crazy. But I need the questions in my head answered. I wonder if she has left yet. I don't want to call her, not yet.

I'm a few roads away from hers, and I realise I can't speak to her, not yet anyway... but I need to know where she is... I call the station.

"Good morning, Paddington Police station..."

"Mark, it's Paul…"

"Hey, you alright?"

"Yeah, I'm good. Quick question: has Nicole come in yet?"

"Umm, yeah, she came in about five minutes ago. Do you want me to transfer you to her?" he asks.

"No, it's okay, I'll speak to her when I get in. Thanks," I hang up before he can answer.

Knowing that she's not anywhere close and a good 20 minutes away, I pull up outside her place and get out of my car.

I walk past her gate and start up her stairs. I scan the street around me to see if I have any onlookers. There's no one around except a single jogger with large headphones on her head and a couple smiling and talking to each other as they walk past; I don't see anyone else on the street. This gives me the confidence I need. As I reach her door, I quickly pull out my lock pick. This is beyond me. On a normal day, I'd have said that this was disobeying the law in the highest order. Entering a property without a warrant is one of the worst things I could be doing, but this isn't a normal day, I just want to know if my friend is who she says she is.

My brother, Richie, taught me all he knew about lock picking. Let's just say I wasn't always a law-abiding citizen, so I open the door on my first try. I step in and close it behind me. As expected, her sitting room is bland. When I say bland, I mean that it is beyond sparse. There is no chair, nor is there a table. Only a mat with a miniature table at the centre. Is this some minimalist shit or some Asian-inspired decoration? I glance over this for a while and walk into the room, inspecting the rest of it. There isn't much I can see from here, but I wade in to search for anything I can find.

I don't underestimate Nicole. She is one of the smartest people I know. And if it is true that she is the killer, then she'd not keep anything that would implicate her here. We are both detectives. We know the rules like the back of our hands. She will try to distance herself from any entanglement with her colleagues, with me. This, for a moment, makes me really think: Should I be here? But a sensation deep inside me makes me continue to progress into the flat.

When I enter the bedroom, which is as sparse as the rest of the room except her bed, I try to begin my search. In my mind, I am already counting down the time. There is a chance that Nicole could return at any moment. The bedroom is filled with a wardrobe, a cupboard, a shelf, her bed, and a vanity table with mirror and make-up, which I am sure she has never used. This is all for decoration. Nicole never wears make-up; she doesn't need it. All of this is for show; I know when a scene has been staged.

I quickly start searching the room. I open the wardrobe first. Killing off my decency, I shove apart her clothes, which consist of suits, shirts, black pants or jeans, jumpers, dresses, gym wear, the normal wardrobe of a young woman. Everything is colour-coded to the tenth power. All of these are things I expect to see in a wardrobe, so I don't make any conclusions yet. Instead, I continue searching. I move down to her footwear, and not surprisingly, I see heels, flats, boots, trainers of several types. But I notice something as I glance over them. She has multiples of the same black pair, in fact. This isn't something that is damning, but the words of Theresa still echo in my mind. I move to the chest of drawers and open the top one; I quickly shut it because I see her lace underwear neatly folded in it.

But my search isn't done yet.

I move along to the second drawer, and inside is an assortment of T-shirts and vest tops; again, nothing untoward or unusual. I'm letting my mind run away with me. Could this be a waste of time? I start to put back some of the items that I pulled out of the drawer and notice that the depth of the drawer does not match the level at where the base is inside. That is weird. I take out all the clothes in the drawer and put them on the bed. Under one of the piles of clothes is a small stack of envelopes. I flick through them, and nothing stands out; a few bills and bank statements, and there is a white envelope with Nicole's name and address handwritten. I turn it over and on the back is a return address and name, her mother's. I put these aside with the clothes I took out.

I try and pull the drawer out further, but it won't come all the way out. I feel around the inside of the drawer to see if there is a way of lifting the base; nothing. I move my hands to the sides and feel around the edges; no luck, nothing. I run my hands underneath at the front, and once again there is nothing... What is this? At the back of the drawer is a small hole, big enough for you to push your finger in. I push my index finger inside, and the base of the drawer pops up. Well, look at that.

What are you hiding, Nicole?

I push down on one side of the bottom of the drawer so that the other side lifts, and I can remove what I realise is a false bottom... a hidden compartment. I feel like I have been hit by a train. Inside is fitted with what looks like foam inserts for gift boxes. However, there is no gift inside. What is there are medical tools. WHAT THE FUCK!! There are several scalpels, all varied in size. Needles, vials with different colour liquids in them and an array of other instruments that all look sharp and could be dangerous in the wrong hands.

My throat feels like it's closing up. This can't be true. All those people!?! That little boy. A CHILD?! A GODDAMN CHILD, NICOLE!! Why? How could you do those things? I have so many questions running through my head right now.

I quickly pull out my phone, activate my camera screen, and snap a few pictures, including the envelope with her mother's address, carefully making sure not to touch anything more than I have to. I also make sure I put them back precisely as they were before. I replace the false bottom in the drawer, making sure to push it back down into place, and I put the clothes I removed earlier back and shut the drawer. I move back to the wardrobe and take photos of the contents inside. I need to be fast. I need to get back to the station. We are, after all, in the middle of a case.

I'm done. I try my best to make sure I return everything back to the way they were when I entered. I heave a breath and then start to get out of there. As I make it out of her house, I am still thinking of what I am going to do with what I now know. It's not enough evidence, but for me, it is still something. I don't know what to think. Is Nicole really who we have been looking for? Bloody hell, I curse under my breath. She has been there all along, investigating herself. She's been right under our noses the whole time. I should have seen the signs. It's my job too. It has been my job for the last decade. How could I have been so blind?

I can't move forward with this little evidence, though. With no warrant. all of this is inadmissible in court, not to mention the whole breaking and entering thing. I need to find a way of telling Pangborn without Nicole catching on. If spooked, she might hightail it out of the city, country even, if she suspects anything. No. I need more than this, I need to catch her in the act. That would be the hard evidence I'd need. This consoles me. At least now I have an action plan. I just need to play along and see if she slips up somehow.

Successfully pulling this off will be hard. Nicole is one of the smartest, if not the smartest person I know. To have done what she has is no small task. The planning that must have gone behind each act would have had to be so precise. She had everything accounted for. Everything other than a nosy old lady.

As I walk back to my car, I can feel a headache start to creep in. I try to ignore it the best I can. As I get in, I try and shake it off. I need answers, and I need them now. I can probably buy myself a few more hours before I need to head into the station. I start the car and type in an address into the satnav. It's going to take 45 minutes to an hour at the least to get there. It's time to get some of my questions answered.

Chapter Twenty-Four

I'M HOME

Nicole

Something is wrong. I sniff the air and slowly look around. Something is wrong. I enter my flat slowly and pull out my service weapon from the holster. A Glock 17. I pull the safety catch and slowly close the door with my left foot. I sniff the air again. Do you know something about scents? They tell us who and what you are. Research shows that dogs have roughly 40 times more smell-sensitive receptors than humans. They can smell the scent of animals, humans, plants, and other things from leagues away. My point is, it is possible to increase your sense of smell just by practicing, and that's exactly what I did when I was younger.

When I was younger and when I went to university, I had two German shepherds that patrolled my flat every day. I would watch and study how they move, how they would start to bark just by sniffing the change of scents in the air as someone approached my home. After conducting some research, I learned that it is possible to increase my sense of smell with practice. You can do this by smelling something, concentrating on it and connecting that smell to either a person, place or thing.

That is how I know that the air in my room smells different. It smells like all the medium-to-less quality perfume used around London, either by male or female. I can't put my hands on which one. Trust me, I know most of them. I have them even. But I know I have smelt this one before. I just can't put my finger on it, but I know it is going to come to me. It's just a matter of time. That, however, isn't the problem. The problem right now is someone has been in here.

Someone was crazy enough to come into my house, break into my house even. I look around my living room, and I am quick to realise that none of my furniture is missing. I don't let up a relieved sigh yet. I still have reservations that this is no common theft.

Someone was in here, though. I know off the bat I can rule out my landlord; he's not been anywhere inside this place since I moved in. The closest he's come is standing at the front door to hand me the rent increase letter once a year.

I quickly step away from the living room and make my way to my dining area and see that nothing is amiss there too. I turn to head towards my bedroom, the muzzle of my Glock leading the way, and I slowly open the door. Sniffing the air again, I catch the same scent. It is denser here. Whoever was in my flat was in here the longest; the door being closed kept the air in the room.

And now, as I inhale the scent again, something registers in my mind. Of course. I know where I'd smelt that before. I know who it belongs to. Bloody fucker. The scent is none other than Paul. Why the hell was he in my house? I scan my room and see that everything is still in the same way I left it. But I know that he's been inside my room. I wonder what made him come here. The fucker had told me he had an appointment and was going to be coming into work late. I overheard Mark talking to another officer and telling him that he was going to see some woman called Theresa. Why did he lie? What reason would he have to come here?

I hate it when people lie to me. I hate it the more when they start suspecting me. And I detest the fact that he went behind my back to search my home. It tells me things, and it makes me want to do things like. . . like address my snooping partner.

I don't try to think about what this Theresa has told him. For him to come to my home and search it the way he did, then that means he knows or suspects that I'm the killer. Well, kudos to you, Paul. Never knew you had it in you. Seems like I have far underestimated you. I need to be on the lookout for any possible setup on the way now.

A thought comes to me now. To call him. To know how his interview with Theresa went. I'm trying to gauge the proximity of his attack with what he knew. But I hold myself. There is no need for that. We will still meet tomorrow or next, because someone is definitely going to die again. No. I need to know what he knows, and the kind of measures I'd need to put in place for him.

I move over to my wardrobe and see that my clothes are still arranged the way I left them. No. Scratch that. I do notice a change. You've got to have an eye for detail in things. I see my black T-shirts and trousers are too far apart from my other clothes. Hmm. He searched here. I don't pull them together; instead, I close the wardrobe. Where else did he look? Yes. The shoes next. I open the compartment below the wardrobe and observe my collection. It hasn't been tampered with, but I know that he looked at it. Fucker. What was he looking for?

Next, I pull open my drawer housing my undies. I'm not surprised it's the way I left it. The white and black lace underwear are neatly folded in the compartment. It wasn't even touched. I guess Paul's decency got the best of him.

I open the drawer below that's filled with T-shirts and other items of clothing. Nothing looks out of place here... Wait, those T-shirts are in the wrong place. He couldn't have... I pull all the clothes out, throwing them on the floor. I take out the letters that I keep under them. They're not in the order that I normally leave them in. The letter from my mother is at the bottom of the pile. This is not how I left it. All the envelopes are normally kept in size order, smallest to biggest. I chuck the letters on the bed and pull the drawer out further. I reach underneath and insert my finger into the hole in the back to release the latch, and I pull the false base up and look at the contents. Everything is still there. Nothing's been touched. Wait, one of the vials isn't all the way down in its compartment. I pull out a pair of medical gloves from my jacket pocket, put them on and take the bottle out. It hasn't been opened; it has, however, been touched; there is a smudge on the bottle.

You touched it bare-handed. You idiot. You should know better than that, Paul.

Looking at the bottle, then the letters, more specifically the one from my mother, I realise what he's about to do. It looks like they are finally going to meet, after all.

Shaking my head with a smile on my face; so predictable. Granted, I would have done the same thing, only I would make sure that I don't leave my fingerprints on anything. I pull out a handkerchief, carefully wrap the bottle in it, and put it in my pocket.

I look around the room. Great, now I have to clean up this mess... actually, it will come in handy if I leave it this way.

What's the time? 12:20pm damn, it takes less than an hour to get to hers from here, depending on the traffic. If he was here this morning, he would already be there or possibly might have left already. Either way, it doesn't matter.

Damn you, Paul, why couldn't you just mind your own and not go snooping? Even if you were, why did you have to bring other people into it? I need to find out what she's told you. I hope to God that you haven't said anything Susanne, for your own good, I really hope that you haven't.

Only one way to find out I guess, looks like our monthly visit is going to have to be pushed up. I pull out a small bag from the drawer and pack a few essentials. I really don't want to have to do anything, but there is no way that I can leave anything to chance. I need to get Theresa's address.

As I go to leave my bedroom, I pull out my phone and open the tracker app I have installed. I guess he doesn't remember that we have this installed. A long time ago, I managed to hack the app so that it wouldn't give the right location for me if I was searched. However, I could see where he was and where he's been. Never thought to use it before; there was no reason. I've never been overly interested in his life to care enough to use it. I guess today is the day I put it to use. The log for his car registration for today shows his home address, the station, mine, Susanne's and another. Hello, Theresa. I think I have a few visits to make before I head back to the station.

Chapter Twenty-Five

TRUTH

Paul

"Thank you, ma'am," I say as I accept a cup of hot coffee from Nicole's mother.

She waves it off and smiles. "Been a long time since someone has called me that."

I give her a sheepish grin. "That's because you don't go out lately."

She nods. "Could be."

I sip the coffee. I'm surprised it tastes much better than some of the ones I get at Starbucks.

Mrs Susanne Murphy clocks my expression and smiles. She asks, "Like it?"

I nod and say, "Love it."

She giggles. "You have to thank my husband Ignacio for that," she says, then places her left hand on her chest and adds softly, "bless his soul. He was one the best coffee makers around back in the day. He even had a few coffee shops around London." She pauses and closes her eyes as if to remember some far-off thoughts. "He was so successful that we used to spend our vacations in different exotic places around the world. It was fun while it lasted."

She pauses here. Her eyes are still closed, and her hands are still placed on her chest.

I don't know what to say, but I know that I need to say something, so I just ask, "And what happened?"

Her eyes open, and she shakes her head. "Broken heart, I think, is what it is called in layman's terms... It's a long story. Don't mind me. I'm so used to bothering my friends and loved ones with stories that I ended up chasing them away."

"I'm not in any way bothered, ma'am," I say.

This elicits a hearty laugh from her. "You're sweet," she says, and then adds, "But that's enough about me." She waves it off and then fixes me with a withering gaze. "You said on the phone you wanted to talk about Nicole."

I nod. "Yes, ma'am."

"You say you and Nicole are partners. . ."

"Yes, we work together."

"Yes," she says, nodding as if she is ticking off something from her head.

"What do you want to know about Nicole?" she asks, her gaze still fixed on me.

"Um. . ." How to begin. I've been racking my brain on the drive here to come up with how I will phrase the questions to her. Certainly, she's still smart enough to know if I was phoney and just came to retrieve as much information as I can to use against her daughter. But I couldn't get anything off my head. Everything I've got sounds phoney. I clear my throat and try again. "I just wanted to know about Nicole. What she was like growing up and all."

Susanne still has her eyes glued to me as she asks, "She hasn't been forthcoming with herself with you, has she?" I don't know how she knew this. Well, a mother knows her child best, right? But I just shake my head.

She cocks her head to the side and asks. "Why do you want to know about her?"

I blink and play with my lips a little, thinking of a suitable answer. I can see the woman scrutinising me. Any wrong answer, and she knows I am phoney. I say, "I don't want to lie to you, ma'am. You seem like an intelligent woman."

She nods at this and smiles. "If you say so."

"The reason I want to know is that Nicole has been exhibiting a certain kind of behaviour lately that quite frankly has me a little worried. I found something of hers that makes me think she's hiding something. I'm scared that she might be involved in something that she shouldn't be..."

Susanne asks suddenly. "Are you in the middle of an investigation, son?"

I'm too shocked by this. I simply answer with a nod.

"Thought so," Susanne says. Then she adds, "And Nicole is working with you?"

Again, I nod. Where is this going?

She shrugs. "A mother is meant to protect their child." She fixes her gaze on me again. "I believe it was William Makepeace Thackeray who once said, 'Mother is God in the eyes of a child.' We sacrifice everything for our children's happiness. When a child is hurt, no matter what age they are, they always want their mother. When they're in trouble, it's always Mum."

Her eyes have a slight mist to them, like she's about to start crying. She shakes this away and continues. "A mother's job is to protect their child... sometimes we do this even when we know they are wrong."

She sips her coffee and says, "Nicole is an only child, and as an only child, Ignacio and I tried to give her everything she wanted. She went to the best schools, moved in all the right circles, she had anything and everything she wanted. We gave her everything. And she made us proud too. She's so smart, so smart, too smart, in fact." She sounds somewhat sorrowful.

I lean back in my chair, giving her space to continue talking.

"Her father and I had her tested when she was younger; her English teacher suggested it. Said that she was extremely intelligent for her age... turned out intelligent was a slight understatement."

Nicole never really talked about her younger self; she sure as hell never said that she was from a well-off family. Actually, from the sounds of it and the look of her mother's home, I would say upper-middle class family. Our conversation rarely went past our investigations. I just put it down to her being private, which is fair, not everyone wants to talk about themselves. It used to bother me a few years into us working together, but then I got used to it.

Susanne continues. "They said she has an IQ of around 190. Thinks and sees the world different from me and you. Just as the way she processes it." She stops and sips her coffee. I drink mine too. I have a feeling she's about to arrive at something, so I just wait for her to do that.

Susanne says, "I noticed the changes when she turned 16. It was subtle, but it was there. She wanted to have control." She laughs at this and says, "She and her father used to fight a lot about that. We'd have to remind her that we were her parents. She had a way with people that was somewhat amazing to watch; that is when we caught on to what she was doing. The way she would play her father and I against each other. Not because she wanted something, you know, the way most children would. Ask Mum for something, and when she would say no, go to Dad and get him to say yes or vice versa. She would manage to start these arguments that almost drove us to divorce on more than one occasion. She had fun toying with people."

What the. . . Was there ever a time that she tried to do this to me? Made me do what she wanted just for the fun of it. I don't remember much. But something tells me that she's done it to me more than once.

"She developed a strange fascination with medicine. Her bedroom was filled with books, spent hours online looking and reading up on different things. We thought it was just a random interest. Or possibly a career path..."

She looks out the window and gives a small chuckle.

"I would say that the world is very lucky that she didn't." Susanne looks back at me as if the weight of the world is on her shoulders. It's clear that she loves her daughter, but there's something else there too... I can't put my finger on it.

"We should have kept more of an eye on her, should have had her see someone, a professional. Her father and I weren't equipped to deal with her. I guess we also didn't want anyone else to know – that whole family business is family business..."

Her voice suddenly changes. I watch her eyes start to mist.

What did you do, Nicole?

She gets up and walks over to the desk at the end of the room, opens one of the drawers, shuffles through the contents, and pulls out a file. She opens it and looks at me. Like she's fighting internally with herself. She takes a deep breath, walks back to where we're sitting, and sits back down, holding the file to her chest. She takes another deep breath, places the file on the coffee table, and slides it over to my direction. I guess she made up her mind.

I put my coffee cup on the table and pick the file up. I look back up at her as she wipes a small tear from her eye.

"When she was around 16 or 17, She had this friend, Amelia Watkins. She was one of the very few people that you could say Nikky had somewhat of a relationship with. I think on Amelia's part it was true, to a point, then it became more out of fear."

I flick through the pages in the file that she gave me. They are all newspaper clippings that have gone slightly yellow with age.

"They had a sleep over at Amelia's house, and something happened. Her parents were out of the country in the south of France or Italy, somewhere. It wasn't a big deal, they often stayed over with each other when one set of parents went out of the country. Ignacio and I never thought anything of it, Amelia was a very nice girl…"

I look up at her as I think to myself, *was…*

"Amelia had recently broken up with her boyfriend, and according to Nikky, he hadn't taken it well. She said that he had turned up to the house that evening and tried to get back with Amelia, brought flowers, chocolates and some wine, the usual `I'm sorry` arrangement that you young fellas try and woo us women with."

I chuckle a little at this, nodding. I know that's a move I've tried in the past.

Suanne shares a warm smile with me as she catches me reminiscing. Her smile slowly leaves as she continues.

"According to Nicole, Amelia and the young man… I can't recall his name; it should be in one of those clippings."

She gestures to the file in my hands.

"They get into an argument, and she tells him to leave. He apparently refuses and gets physical with her. Nicole says that she got in the middle of them and threatened to call the police if he didn't leave. She said that he pushed her into a table that the Watkins had in their hallway, shouting at them."

She picks up her coffee cup, looking into it as if she was studying something floating in the latte-coloured liquid.

"This caused the neighbours to come out and knock on the door to check on the girls."

I look at her to continue.

"They say that they watched him leave the building, and one of them even followed him down and told the concierge not to let him back in the building. They said that they didn't hear anything from the girls for the rest of the night, other than the TV and music."

Where is she going with this?

"The concierge told the police in the morning that no one had been back into the building that night but that he saw that the young man had sat across the street for some time. About an hour or more, then he left."

Wait, what? "The police?"

Suanne nods. "Yes, neighbours called in the morning when they heard screaming coming from the flat. They had the morning concierge open the door. Nicole was in Amelia's room holding her; they say she looked like a rag doll being rocked back and forth. Have you seen those old-school rag dolls with plaited wool hair? The ones with button eyes?"

"Yes, I have." My cousin had loads of them when we were younger; they used to freak me out with their sewn-in eyes...

"Yeah, well, imagine what one would look like with their buttons missing and the thread still poking out of where they would have been. That's what they found when they went into the room."

My head is spinning. There is no way that Nicole could have done that, would have done that to her friend.

"After the police arrived and took Nicole's statement about what happened the night before, they went looking for the ex-boyfriend..."

"Were they able to speak to him?" I ask. I wipe my palm on my trouser leg, leaving a slightly damp patch.

"No. They tracked his phone to some park, where he had sent a text to his parents saying that he was sorry. He was sat on a bench when they found him. He had taken something and died from an overdose. He was apparently covered in blood. There should be something in there giving a bit more detail."

I turn the pages of the file in front of me and come to a page about a body found in Primrose Hill.

This morning police were called to Primrose Hill in Camden. Where the body of a teenager was found. Even though the clothes of the victim were covered in blood, it has been reported that the blood was not that of the victim. The only items found on the victim were a mobile phone, wallet and some sort of weapon.

As of right now the police are not releasing the name of the victim until they speak with the family. They are investigating whether this could be linked to the death of an eighteen-year-old girl that took place late last night.

My head feels heavy, like it's filled with water. She can't be really telling me that she thinks Nicole did those things.

"You think Nicole had something to do with their deaths?"

"When the police interviewed her, she told them about going over to Amelia's for the night. That the young man turned up a few hours later. She told them about the argument that happened. Which the neighbours backed up. She told them that she had taken some pills because her side had started to hurt, from where he had thrown her into the table and knocked her out for the night. That she didn't wake up till the following morning and found Amelia in her room."

Suanne pauses a bit to catch her breath.

"Her father and I end up going into a hyper-protective mood over her. Wouldn't let her go anywhere unless one of us was with her or there were going to be adults around... she didn't seem to mind, though she ended up spending most of her days before heading off to university in her room or about the house with her nose in a book."

She takes another deep breath and finishes off the coffee in her cup. She places it on the table and leans back in her chair and looks me dead centre in the eyes.

"About a month later, I was doing some washing and was putting some of her clothes away, when I went into her wardrobe. My hand hit something glass on the back of the shelf. Being the typical mum, I pulled it out... I wish to God I hadn't."

I can feel the sorrow in her voice to know it's going to be something terrible.

"I pulled out a glass jar, which had some sort of liquid and a pair of bright hazel eyes looking back at me."

I try to talk, but no sound comes out. I feel like I'm giving her my best impression of a fish gasping for air.

Tears fall from her eyes as she continues, "Ignacio must have been calling me because the next thing I know, he had taken the jar out of my hand and was running down the stairs to the study where Nicole had been reading. Funny enough, she was reading a book on criminal law. I ran down after him and could hear him asking, 'What is this? Tell me what it is! Where are they from.' You would have thought that he was asking her what the colour of the sky was. With no hesitation, she so matter of factly said, 'They're Amelia's,' and continued reading her book."

Finally finding my voice, I ask, "What did you do?"

"What do you mean, what did we do?" She has a questioning tone to her voice.

"Your daughter had human organs hidden in her room from her dead friend... What did you do!" I don't mean to shout, but I can't believe that she just asked me that question.

At that moment I see where Nicole gets at least one part of her personality from. Her mother stands abruptly and stares me down with her piercing green eyes that almost seem to be burning with fire behind her glasses.

She walks over to the window and looks out at the street below us. "We did what we had to... to protect our daughter."

I can't believe she's saying this. I can't believe what I've just learnt over the last hour.

"Protect your daughter?! You didn't protect your daughter; you protected a murderer."

I stand and walk over to where she stands.

"You don't have children, do you?" She sounds worn down, like all her energy has been drained from her body.

"No, I don't," I answer, still looking at her side profile. She hasn't looked at me since I stepped next to her. I don't know what she's looking at, and I don't care.

"I hope you have children one day; you seem like a good man. I pray you do. Cause only then will you know how it feels to be a parent; only then will you know what you would do to protect your family."

My anger at her has subsided a little, and some part of me can understand why she never told anyone what Nicole did. However, I then see the photos in my case file on my desk of the people she's killed. Those innocent people that did nothing to her. The little boy who should be running around playing football. His little face flashes in my mind's eye. His little chubby face. Then I remember what she did to him. How she left him staged in his room as if he was playing with his toys. All the anger that had somewhat gone came roaring back like a fire that had been stoked.

"I know one thing for sure, no matter how much I love my children, I will never allow them to hurt others. Because of you and your husband, five people, one of which is a child, have been killed, and that's five that we know of. God only knows how many people she has actually killed."

A barrage of questions starts swamping my mind. How many others have there been? Did we investigate any? We couldn't have, or we would have linked them to these by now. Maybe they were investigated by different stations? Did we have closed cases where we pinned other people for her crimes? My head starts thumping.

"You're going to have to come to the station with me..."

For the first time in around five minutes, she looks at me and, with a straight face, asks, "Why would I do that?"

You have got to be joking, right, woman?!

"To make an official report..."

"I most definitely won't be doing that, young man."

We stand there looking at each other like we both have grown a second head.

"You have no choice; I have evidence right there on your coffee table..."

"You have newspaper clippings, glowing school reports and a Mensa certificate... you have nothing."

"I have your story..." I counter with.

"You do? Do you have it recorded? You don't have anyone else here to corroborate your apparent findings."

Shit! she's right. I keep my poker face on, hoping that it will make her crack.

"Actually, you might have caused yourself a bit of a problem."

I tilt my head slightly, and she mirrors my move.

"How did you get here? I know Nicole never told you where I live? I'm not listed anywhere. Have you been stalking my daughter, detective? You force me to go anywhere, and you are going to have a lot to explain."

She's right. I can't do a damn thing with anything that I've found out; it's all circumstantial, if that.

While I've been in my head, she has moved to the living room doorway and is standing waiting for me. I guess I have overstayed my welcome.

I sigh and shake my head with frustration but don't say anything as I move past her to the hallway and towards the front door. She walks silently behind me. I open the door and stand on the front step.

"Please, Mrs Murphy, I know you love your daughter, I really do. However, you must help me; you have to help her. She can't keep doing what she's doing. She needs help. No one will think badly of you if you help us convict her. Surely, if the roles were reversed and Nicole was one of victims, if she was Amelia, you would want whoever hurt her brought to justice."

She looks at me with a sad smirk and shakes her head.

"You're right. If the situation was different, I would... However, it's not. Good day, Detective."

And with the she shuts the door in my face,

Chapter Twenty-Six

HELLO, MOTHER

Nicole

The timing is almost perfect; it's taken me just under 50 minutes to get here. I could see my mother's living room window from where I had parked my car. I had chosen a spot a little further up the street on the opposite side of the road, giving me a better vantage point. The sunlight filtered through the trees and illuminated the surrounding houses, casting a warm glow over the neighbourhood. The faint sounds of children playing and dogs barking added to what would have been considered an idyllic scene. My heart pounded in anticipation as I waited for my target to make an appearance.

As I sit in my car outside the house, I can't help but wonder if Paul is still inside. Has he already come and gone? My eyes quickly scan the road, searching for any sign of his car. And then I see it, parked just in front of the house.

I let out a deep sigh, feeling a mix of frustration and sadness. What could Suanne have possibly said to him? Why couldn't he just mind his own business? Now, because of his meddling, two people's lives who were never going to be on my radar are going to be cut short. After my visit to my dear old mother, I'm going to have to pay Mrs Theresa a visit.

I need a way into the house. Walking through the front door would be too risky, but there is a side alley that leads to the back gardens of the neighbouring houses along this street, and the tenants keep the gate locked for security. But I have always had a key since my teenage years and never returned it after moving out.

Stepping out of my car, I inhale deeply, taking in the crisp, cool air. With a quick check of the window and front door, I lock my car and cautiously cross the street towards the alleyway. My eyes dart around, scanning for any signs of movement as I approach the gate. Carefully donning a pair of medical gloves, I retrieve my keys and locate the one for the gate. As I unlock and push it open, I can hear the faint creaking sound echoing in the empty alleyway. Taking one last glance around, I slip inside and quickly shut and lock the gate behind me.

Thankfully, the residents of the street are mostly elderly and have not yet caught on to the modern trend of installing security cameras, so I know I don't have to worry about potentially being caught on CCTV.

I move stealthily through the narrow alleyway, careful not to make any noise that could give me away. With each step, I count off the back of the houses until I reach my destination. In front of me stands a tall wooden gate leading to the back garden, a barrier between me and my goal. To reach over and unlock it, I grab an old, weathered chair that has been carelessly discarded against the wall and use it as a makeshift step. I balance precariously on the chair and reach for the latch on the other side.

The door unlocks, and I'm greeted by the picturesque back garden with every leaf pinched and pruned to perfection.

As I walk through the garden, I take in the scent of lavender and rosemary that fills the air. I used to hate the mixture of the two scents when I was younger. Now, there is something oddly soothing about them.

I walk up the garden steps that lead from the kitchen down to the spotless patio. I push down on the door handle, and the door quietly slides open; I take another look around to make sure that no one is around and slip in.

As I close the door behind me, my senses are immediately overwhelmed by the familiar sights and scents of my mother's kitchen. The air is filled with the aroma of freshly brewed coffee, wafting from my father's old caffettiera sitting next to the gleaming six-burner gas stove. In the centre of the island stands a crystal vase brimming with vibrant flowers freshly picked from the garden.

Leaving the kitchen, I make my way down the hallway towards the living room at the front of the house. I can hear two voices in conversation as I approach. Mother's voice sounds strained, though I can't make out the exact words being spoken. The door to the dining room is slightly open, so I push it further and enter the room, gently closing the door behind me. I position myself between the door and a section of the wall that juts out into the living room, using it as cover as I listen to their conversation.

"Why would I do that?" I hear my mother ask. This no doubt annoys Paul, as when he answers, his voice is slightly on edge. One thing I will say that I get from my mother is my stubbornness, which is for sure pissing Paul off. It used to have us at loggerheads when I was younger, until she learnt that it was not only easier letting me have my way but also safer.

I hear the sound of heels coming closer to where I'm standing and can smell Mother's Elizabeth Arden perfume. She's standing on the other side of the wall. Ten inches of wall and plaster divide us. I hear another set of footsteps, which sound a little heavier; this has to be Paul.

The second set of footsteps continue walking and is followed by the sound of heels clicking on the parquet flooring. Thankfully, they are heading towards the front door.

I step out from behind the wall and into the living room, and as I could have guessed, Mother has been the ever-attentive hostess. Her best coffee cups and saucers sit on the dark oak coffee table, along with all the fixings to go with them inside the service tray. Sugar bowl, milk pot, sterling silver teaspoons and a plate of sugar cookies.

Next to the tray, lies an open manila-coloured file. I push some of the papers around, skim-reading some of the paperwork. Why would you keep these?

I think it's time me and Mother dearest have a little chat. I move to sit in the chair that faces both the door and living room window. You can't see it from the outside of the house, so I'm not worried about Paul seeing me.

I pull out my little bag of tricks and lay them on top of the file. As I hear the front door close, I pull out my Glock and non-police-issued silencer and screw it into place.

The sound of heels makes their way back towards me and come to an abrupt stop in the doorway.

"Hello, Mother," I say without looking up, my finger resting on the trigger.

"Nicole," she replies, her tone stern and fearful.

"I think it's time we had a little chat," I state confidently, gesturing towards the file with my weapon.

She doesn't go to move, only looks out of the window and back towards me.

"Please... sit down. I have other places I need to be."

Chapter Twenty-Seven

LET'S PLAY

Nicole

I lay in bed, half expecting the sound of my front door being kicked in at any moment. Images of Paul and Pangborn storming into my home with guns raised flashed through my mind. But to my surprise, that wasn't how the day began.

Instead, I was awakened by the familiar beep of my alarm at 6:30am. With a sigh, I push myself out of bed and walk over to open the curtains in my bedroom. The first rays of sunshine are just starting to peek over the neighbouring houses, casting a warm glow of pink, orange, and yellow rays onto my face.

I wonder what the day is going to bring? After the chat I had with my mother and Theresa, I should be hightailing it to an airport to some exotic paradise that has no extradition laws. I, however, am standing in my bedroom window, enjoying the sunrise.

However, for some reason, I am meditatively calm. I check the time again and head to my bathroom, and start getting ready for the day.

The steam from the shower slowly fills the room as I begin brushing my teeth. The minty freshness of the toothpaste tingles on my tongue before I rinse it away, wondering if this could be the last time I use it. But in a flash, the thought is gone, and I replace the toothbrush back in its holder.

When I step into the shower, hot water cascades over me like a thousand tiny pinpricks against my skin. The scent of mango and strawberry shower gel fills the air as I lather it onto my body, creating a thick white foam that cocoons me. Once fully covered, I step back under the stream of water and let it wash away all traces of lather.

As I make my way back to my bedroom, phone in hand, I check the time once again: 7:00am. With only an hour before I have to leave for work, I quickly get dressed in my usual work attire before heading to the kitchen for my daily dose of morning coffee. The rich aroma fills my senses as I take a sip, preparing myself for the day ahead.

The sound of my phone ringing interrupts my thoughts; I pick it up and look at the name. PAUL ADAMS is slowly moving across the top of the screen. What in the world could he be calling for?

"Hello," I answer as I put the call on speaker and place the phone on the kitchen counter.

"Hey, you up?" Paul asks.

"Up and dressed..." I answer. What does he want? We haven't spoken since yesterday morning. We both had a busy day, so we weren't around each other at all. We briefly saw each other in passing when I got back to the office yesterday, but we didn't have any interaction.

"Okay, cool. I just got a call to go to a scene. They'll probably be calling you too," Paul says.

Almost as if on cue, my phone dings with a new text message. I quickly check the address and realise it's not one that I recognise. It must mean that neither my mother nor Theresa have been reported yet.

"Yeah, just got the text," I say to him.

"Do you want me to pick you up? I'm just walking out the door now."

I side-eye the phone as he talks. What could he be up to?

"Yeah, sure, if you don't mind. I'm literally finishing up my coffee, so just honk when you're outside," I say to him.

"Okay, see you in a few," he says and hangs up the phone.

I look at the phone on the countertop as I finish my coffee and rinse the cup out.

Around 15 minutes later, I hear a car horn and look outside my living room window, and there he is. I signal from the window that I see him, and he nods back in response.

I grab my jacket, badge, keys and gun off the dining room table and head towards the door.

As I open the door, I'm hit by the bright light from the sun. I move back into my flat to grab my sunglasses out of the drawer in my hallway console. I put them on and check my reflection in the mirror. Happy with my look, I go to leave, pulling and locking the door. I see Paul watching me as I come down the stairs and walk to his car.

We haven't said more than a few words to each other since I entered his car. Most of the car ride is in silence. I only interpret it as I read out bits of information about the scene that was sent to us.

It takes us about 50 minutes to get to the address. There are a number of police cars and officers talking to people as we pull up.

Paul parks the car and we both exit. A detective named Charles Haywood breaks away from his conversation with other officers and approaches us. He's wide-set and slightly overweight, his belly threatening to spill over his belt.

He shakes our hands before Paul speaks up. "Sorry if we're intruding – this is your jurisdiction, and we don't want to trespass."

Haywood waves off his concerns. "Not at all. Your chief informed me that you're working on a related case. We wanted to see if there are any connections."

Paul nods. I see his eyes dart towards me and then back at Haywood. "Good thinking"

Haywood gestures towards the building. "Would you like me to take you guys in?"

"Please," Paul says, nodding.

We follow Haywood inside, taking in the remnants of what used to be a shop. As we walk, Paul asks for Haywood's thoughts on the case. "So what do you think happened?"

"We don't have a clear picture yet, but it seems like the victim may have known their attacker. There are bruises around the neck that appear to be fading, and a single stab wound under the arm that caused them to bleed out," Haywood explains.

I scan the interior of the building, taking note of the renovations taking place. "Looks like they were in the middle of refurbishing," I comment, gesturing to the paint cans, dust sheets, and scattered tools.

"The owner was planning on selling it, guess he wanted to fix the place up before putting it on the market," Haywood responds as we all come to a halt in front of the body. The pool of blood makes us wary of getting too close.

I look at the scene in front of me, and all I can think of is... what a mess.

I can sense Paul's gaze on me, but I keep my eyes fixed on the gruesome scene. Sorry, buddy, this isn't one of mine, I say to myself.

Paul begins examining the body, bending down to get a closer look. While Haywood continues prattling on about something, neither of us are really listening.

"Could you step outside for a moment, please?" Paul suddenly asks Haywood.

He seems taken aback by the request, clearly caught off guard. Haywood looks from Paul to me.

I say nothing, just slightly shrug my shoulders at him.

Haywood, realising that he was no longer needed, clears his throat and says, "Umm, I'm going to step outside. Get out of you guys hair; see if I can get the CSI unit to hurry up and get in here." He nods once at me and does the same to Paul and then turns and heads back in the direction we entered.

There is a silence in the room now; I can hear the chatter and noise from outside. All of which isn't important right now.

I look around the room a little, seeing if there is anything of any importance. Actually, doing my job. I look back at Paul and decide to have some fun as I step back to the body.

"Oh, I forgot to tell you earlier... someone broke into my place yesterday," I say as I pull out my notepad and pen and step around the body on the floor. He remains unfazed and continues examining it.

"Really? Are you okay? Did they take anything?" He tries to feign concern, but I see right through it.

"No, nothing was taken. Actually, everything was still in its place," I reply.

Still not making any eye contact with me he asks sceptically, "Then how do you know someone broke in?"

"I have a camera," I say nonchalantly. I catch a brief flicker of surprise in his expression. If I hadn't been watching closely, I would have missed it.

"A camera?" He finally looks up at me with interest. He may have a good poker face, but mine is better. Let's see how he wants to play this game.

"Yeah, I had one installed a few years ago. It's always good to have extra security when you're not home."

Paul stops what he's doing and coolly asks, "Did you report it?"

Asshole. He knows I can't. Not when nothing has been stolen. And also not without freely letting the police into my home. "No, I haven't reported it," I say.

"Why not? You've not got anything you're trying to hide, do you? Let me guess, you're an international bank thief and have millions of pounds stashed in your wardrobe and drawers and need to move it before you make the report, right?" he jokingly asks.

Without missing a beat, I answer, "Nah, I think I'm going to deal with it myself, plus the camera didn't pick up a clear image of the person's face."

He stands up as he asks, "Then what are you going to do?"

"I found a print," I say as I write some notes on my pad. I really don't need to write anything down. But I might as well play the part of the detecting detective.

"A print?" was that a slight tremor in your voice, Mr Adams?

"Yeah, I noticed that they hadn't closed a drawer all the way, so I dusted it on the off chance there was something… turns out that my hunch was right. I gave the print to Forensics this morning before I came here. So hopefully they have something for me when I get back to the station."

I can literally see blood drain from Paul's face. I like the effect I have on him. He quickly recollects himself to say, "I hope that all works out for you."

I move to walk past him and stop so that we're eye to eye. "Come on now, you and I both know there's no case unless we have evidence… Policing 101." I give him a slight smile and nudge him. He gives a small smile back.

Looking back at the body on the floor, I say, "We should probably go see if the neighbours heard anything, then make our way back. There's nothing we can do for him now."

"Except find the person that did this to him," he says as he turns and walks out the front door.

I hear him tell the CSI unit that they can head in. I step to the side to give them space as they come back into the house.

As I turn back, I see Paul moving around the front of his car and opening his door. He looks back at me and signals with his hand for me to hurry up. I jog down the stairs to the house and get in the car just as he presses the start/stop button to turn the car on.

Chapter Twenty-Eight

PUTTING EVERYTHING IN PLACE

Nicole

I have no intention of having the print I found run; there's no reason to. I told Paul a few days ago that I was, when we were at the last crime scene. I was just trying to spook him.

I think I got him. He's been on edge every time I go down to see them, or if they send up a file for me.

We still have other cases and admin we need to work on, mister. I do what I do, but I still like to carry out my job to the best of my ability. Give me some credit.

It's actually been hilarious watching him over the last few days. However, it's time to stop playing; he could turn in what he has at any point, and I need to make sure that I stay one step ahead of him.

Over the last few days, I have been meticulously planning my next move. Going over it over and over again.

My plan requires precise timing and careful execution, so I have spent the last few days doing practice runs and fine-tuning every detail. I have allowed for extra time on both ends in case any unexpected obstacles arise.

I sit across from Paul's flat in one of those rent-by-the-hour cars and have a clear view of his front door. I'm waiting for him to leave.

I'm dressed in my usual work attire so as not to call any attention to myself. I'm not worried about being seen by any of his neighbours, as I have often sat in his car when he has had to run home during the day while we were at work.

I do, however, have gloves on my hands which tightly grip the steering wheel.

A backpack is next to me on the passenger seat. I stare at it now and smile. This bag contains everything that will allow me to continue with my life and sadly help me end his. Inside are the tools of my trade. Everything I've used over the last few months, years even, but that's a whole other story. Well, not everything, because I still have some, which I have carefully hidden now. What I do have with me has all been printed with his fingerprints and other means of DNA that will link him to the murders.

All I need to do is get them into his flat. What is taking him so long..? Aww. There you are. I see him coming out of his home. As usual, he is on the phone. Just as I'm thinking about it, my own phone rings. It's on the dashboard, so I just lean over and pick it up. Paul's breathing is heavy on the line as he says, "Hey, morning, I'm just heading to the gym. Do you want me to pick you up when I've finished?"

I fight to roll my eyes. He's trying to keep everything as normal as possible. You can't play me, mister.

"Nah. It's okay, thanks. I'm driving today," I answer.

He pauses as he gets to his car.

"Really? Okay... I'll see you at the station then."

He puts his phone into his jacket pocket, opens the car door, throws his gym bag in the back seat, and gets in.

I hear his engine as he starts the car and pulls away from the curb, conducting a quick three-point turn and heading down the street. I need to be fast with this. Quickly, I start the car's ignition and softly step on the pedal. I cruise slowly down the street until I reach the front of his home and stop.

I park near the curb and turn off the ignition, grabbing the backpack, I open the door and step out. I see no one on the street, which isn't a surprise as it's still very early. I walk fast to Paul's front door and kneel down. Pulling out my lock pick set, I work on the door and have it open in under five seconds.

This is the first time I'm inside Paul's place, and although I don't have the time to really look around the place, I see that he keeps his things clean. Removing the backpack from my shoulder, I take out files and paperwork regarding the case alongside my own collection of information regarding each victim. Including information on myself and my family. I leave these scattered over his coffee table and his desk in his office, which has his own little evidence board set up. Perfect, thanks, Paul, you've made this just that little bit easier.

I head further into his flat and find his bedroom. When I reach his room, I go in and kneel at the side of his bed and lift his mattress. I carefully place all the items that I have set up under it and carefully put the mattress back in place, fixing the duvet.

I look around his room and see a dirty clothes hamper in the corner. I open the hamper and dig through till I find items that I can use. I pull out a pair of brown slacks and a few pipettes that have been filled with blood from my last two... sorry, Paul's last two victims.

I return the trousers to the hamper and make my way across the room to his collection of shoes. Out of all the pairs, I pick one that is already covered in mud and grass. I take out a small jar of dirt from my mother's garden in my backpack, which has sprigs of rosemary and leaves from the specific lavender plants she grew and press the dirt into the shoes and sprinkle some on the floor where the shoes were, before putting them back.

I have a few more items that I need to place before I leave. I move out of his room and walk along the hallway of the flat, opening the doors to find what I am looking for.

I find what I am looking for just before I reach the kitchen. His airing cupboard has the normal crap. Mop and bucket, Hoover, water tank. I pull out a stack of photos and casually flick through them. They are before and after shots of everyone. My mother and Theresa being the last four on the pile.

I set the backpack down to pull out the last piece of the puzzle. I carefully open the latches on the case and lift up the lid. Inside are my most prized possessions, which I am sadly going to have to give up. Tightly packed in the case are sealed jars with embalming fluid and different coloured eyes staring back.

A flash of memories come flooding back. My left hand hovers slightly over each jar. I don't want to touch anything as I could mess up the prints that I planted on them.

Goodbye, my old friends.

I close the case, pulling the latches back in place, and stretch to push it to the back of the cupboard. Not too far so that it would be missed if the police decide to do their search.

After this, I put the backpack over my shoulder and head for the door. I pull my lock picks back out and lock his front door. I take a look around before I head down the stairs and head towards my car. I scan the streets for any onlooker, my eyes on the windows and doors, checking if there is a nosy neighbour or peeping Tom looking out, but I see no one. I reach my car and get in. I don't start the engine, I still have something else to do from this location.

What just took place in Paul's flat was only a small part of a large puzzle.

Before heading over here, I went to the station. Luckily for me, it wasn't even six am when I arrived, so there wasn't even five people in the building. Thankfully, Mark hadn't arrived yet, so there was no line of questioning when I arrived. I basically had the whole floor to myself as the other departments were on the other floors.

I moved confidently towards Paul's desk, my eyes scanning the entrance for any other arriving detectives. Sitting in his chair, I activated his computer and easily logged in – his password was Emma21Paul, a combination of his own name and his ex's.

From my backpack, I pulled out a small flash drive and plugged it into his computer. Opening one of two folders on the drive, I began to work my magic. The first folder held a program that allowed me to hack into the computer and manipulate the time stamps on any files I uploaded or downloaded. With this tool at my disposal, I began uploading information that we had never uncovered during our investigation.

After double-checking that all the dates lined up perfectly, I glanced at my phone to check the time. In just five minutes, a time-sensitive email with my suspicions about Paul and the reason I didn't bring them to him sooner would be sent from my laptop at home directly to Pangborn. If he was to ever decide to investigate the IP address, it would lead straight back to my home address. I could easily explain this away by saying that I didn't want to bring it up in a place where our conversation could potentially be overheard.

After I saved everything, I was able to leave the station before anyone came in and headed straight here.

Now as I sit in my car, I have one last activity that I need to do. I reach inside my glove compartment and pull out a burner phone. I turn it on and start the voice-changing feature that I have installed.

Now, it's time to stretch my acting skills. I pull up the phone app and dial 999.

"Hello, emergency service operator. Which service do you require? fire, police, or ambulance?" says the operator.

"Police... I need the police," I answer with an urgency to my voice.

"I'll just connect you now," is the last thing I hear from this operator before the line clicks and another voice comes online.

"Good morning. What is the nature of your emergency?"

"I've just seen a man put a woman into a car. She wasn't moving, though I think she might be drugged or drunk. It might be nothing, but it just didn't look right."

"Can you give me the location of where you saw this, please?"

"Yes, yes, it was outside 58 ... no, 60 Queens Gate Terrace."

"Are you able to give a description of the man?" she asks. I can hear the tapping of her keyboard in the background.

"White, mid-forties, maybe late forties. Dark brown hair, about 5'10." I give a vague description of Paul.

"You said that he was putting her into a car. Can you describe the car for me?"

"It looked like a goldish Mercedes-Benz."

"Were you able to get the registration number?" she asks, keys still tapping away.

"Umm. Yeah, I'm looking at it now... It's TJ22HZA... I think he's seen me. I need to go." And I hang up.

I know for a fact that they are going to run the plates, and it will pull up Paul's details.

That, alongside what I sent to Pangborn, is absolutely going to raise some flags.

Chapter Twenty-Nine

CHESS NOT CHECKERS

Paul

My mind is spinning, trying to grasp the nightmare that has become my reality. My body is drenched in sweat, heart pounding against my ribcage as if begging for escape. The world around me feels like it's crumbling, collapsing in on itself with each passing moment. How could I have been so blind, trusting someone who I thought was a friend and colleague for all these years? Now they are my greatest enemy and have turned my life into a living hell. Regret eats at me as I realise how I should have acted sooner and brought what I had found out to Pangborn sooner, but no, I had to wait to collect more evidence. Now it's too late. The damage has been done.

Nicole has played her hand, and as much as I hate her right now, it was a damn good one.

I should have been quicker when she mentioned the break-in. It should have been obvious that she knew it was me all along. Her claim of having a print of the trespasser was a ploy to lure me out.

A few hours ago, when I arrived at the station, Pangborn had summoned me into his office. From the look on his face, I knew it was something serious. He looked angry, disappointed and stressed. He took me to one of the interview rooms and told me that I was being taken off the case and arrested, then suggested that I get hold of a lawyer, a good one, as I was seriously going to need one.

I was too shocked to ask why, then he informed me that he had been sent some damning information. He tossed down a file with a stack of papers. There were photos of the victims, medical information, addresses and other pieces of information.

His words all sounded as if I was underwater; my head instantly started to thump. I tried to argue that I didn't do anything. But he just shook his head and said that he had had some of the IT techs search my computer and that he had sent a team to my flat to search it. He then moved on to ask if I had any idea what they found. I had no idea, so I just shook my head.

I started to protest and say that I hadn't done anything and that I was being set up.

As the words left my mouth. The answer hit me like a truck. Nicole!

Fucking bitch!

Pangborn refused to hear my pleas. He just told me that there would be an internal investigation and that I was to stay in this room and not say a word to anyone.

I've sat in this room many a time, conducting my own interviews. The room seems so different from this side of the table. It feels smaller; it feels like the heating is on. I have to get out of here. I can't let her get away with this.

Pangborn isn't going to let me just walk out of the building. This is going to get worse before it gets better. I need to get to the photos I took at Nicole's. Then what? How am I going to prove that what I found belonged to her?

I could tell them that they need to speak to her mother. Maybe she might have a change of heart when she's shown what her daughter has done.

First things first. I need to get out of here. The door to the room opens, and as Pangborn enters the room with a glass of water, I seize my chance and charge past him, ignoring his protests. As I dart down the hallway, my heart pounds against my ribcage as I bound down the eight flights of stairs.

The building alarm blares in my ears.

I can hear Pangborn and others shouting from above, urging me to stop and not be foolish. But there's no turning back now. I've already started running, signing my own death sentence. The only way out of this is to find proof that Nicole is the mastermind behind it all. My mind races with thoughts as I sprint through the corridors. Lost in my racing thoughts, I collide with someone, and we both tumble to the floor. Shaking off the impact, I look up, and who do I see? Nicole herself.

"You! You bitch! What have you done?!" I scream at her, pouncing on top of her and grabbing her shirt collar.

The sudden blow and fall take her by surprise, and she looks slightly shocked, but then her expression shifts to one of amusement as she teases me with a smile.

"What are you talking about?" she asks innocently, tilting her head like a puppy.

Without hesitation, I reach back and punch her square in the jaw. Her smug smile pushes me over the edge.

"Don't act stupid with me, Nic. I know it's you. I know you killed all those people. You planted everything on my laptop, I don't know how, but I know you did it." My whole body shakes with anger as I look down at her.

"I spoke to your mother. I know all about Amelia and what you did to her and her boyfriend. I'll make her talk; she has no choice."

She scratches frantically at my hands, trying to break free from my grasp, but it only fuels my anger, and I hold on tighter.

The sounds of approaching footsteps from above send a surge of panic through me. Time is running out. I glance up to see Pangborn and his team making their way down the stairs, getting closer by the second.

When I look back down at Nicole, her face has transformed from feigned innocence to a sinister smile that sends shivers down my spine. "You're going to have a hard time doing that," she sneers.

A wave of dread washes over me as she speaks.

"What... what have you done?" My tough guy act falters as fear creeps into my voice.

She leans in closer, a malevolent gleam in her eye. "Me? Nothing. But you..." She trails off before dropping the bombshell. "You killed your partner's elderly mother as a warning for her to back off after she found out that you killed the person who saw you with one of your victims."

The shock paralyses me, unable to believe the depths of her deceit. She takes advantage of my momentary weakness and pushes me back.

"By now, there are probably 10 officers tearing through your place, finding all the little 'gifts' I left behind," she taunts, her eyes darker than I've ever seen them.

As our gazes lock, it feels like I'm staring into a void filled with pure malice and evil. I have never been afraid of anyone before in my life. Until now.

Suddenly, Nicole starts screaming. Jolting me out of my dazed state.

The sound of approaching footsteps on the stairs sends a surge of panic through me – they're only two flights away now.

With one final glance at Nicole, I release her shirt, push past her and sprint towards the exit. Adrenaline surges through my veins, pushing me faster and harder. I burst through the door and tear across the car park towards my car, every step fuelled by fear and desperation. I need to get away.

My fingers fumble with the key fob, finally unlocking my car from a few feet away. As I fling myself into the driver's seat, Pangborn's voice echoes through the empty parking lot.

"PAUL, STOP! DON'T MAKE US SHOOT!"

I look back and see him standing at the exit door with a group of officers and detectives, each one armed and ready to fire. For a brief moment, I consider surrendering. But then my eyes fall on Nicole, positioned like a queen on a chessboard, with her pawns and king in front of her, all ready to be sacrificed at her will. Suddenly, giving up is not an option. I slam on the gas and peel out of the car park, leaving Pangborn and the others in my rearview mirror chasing after me.

Chapter Thirty

STAY ON THE LINE.
HELP IS ON ITS WAY

Nicole

My father's dying words were a reminder that we are the main characters in our own story and that it's up to us to shape our own ending. He hoped that his last advice would inspire me, his only child, to change my ways before it was too late. And although my life could have come crashing down a few days ago, fate seemed to be on my side.

If Paul had been cleverer, he would have taken the little information he had straight to Pangborn. But luckily for me, his procrastination gave me the opportunity to make my moves. I could have let things play out with him being indicted for the multiple murders. But unfortunately, unlike our cousins across the pond who have the death penalty, we do not. This means a lengthy prison sentence, something I cannot allow. The last thing I need is some ambitious lawyer trying to make a name for themselves by taking on his case and digging up more evidence.

Throughout the years, I've always had contingency plans in place just in case something like this were to happen. Never did I think that this would be how it would have to end.

The only way to bring this chapter to a close... Paul has to die. It's the only option I have. Him being alive would complicate things for me immensely. Paul needs to be brought to a stop in the most dramatic way possible. So, the city knows that they no longer need to worry about the murderer who has been terrorising it.

After the little fiasco at the station, I told Pangborn that I needed some time to myself. He sent me home, informing me to stay there until he had contacted me. He said that a few officers would be posted outside my flat within the hour. Thankfully, I was able to get home and stage the flat to look as if I had been attacked and kidnapped before anyone had time to arrive.

Under one of my many aliases, I had rented a Zipcar filled with all the necessary props for Paul's final showdown. For hours now, I had been following his every move. He seemed lost and uncertain, constantly on the move as if trying to figure out his next step. He couldn't return home, not with the police and tech teams swarming around it.

Where are you headed, Paul? This place... doesn't seem familiar. Have you been keeping secrets from me? Then again, who am I to judge when I have so many secrets of my own.

As we pull into a dead-end cul de sac, I come to a stop at the top of the road while he continues down to the very end. He slows down in front of a house with boarded-up windows and faded Sitex on the door. Pulling the car into the driveway, I glance up and down the empty street, not seeing any sign of life. The time on my phone reads 10:03pm. It seems that most people are out enjoying the nice weather we've been having lately. This may be my only chance to make a move.

I quietly push open my car door and carefully shut it behind me. Keeping my eyes on him and scanning the surrounding houses, I make my way closer to his car. He turns off the engine and begins to exit the vehicle, glancing around as if sensing someone's presence. Fortunately, he doesn't see me from where I have crouched in the shadows. He moves towards the front door of the abandoned house, fiddling with his keys to unlock the Sitex door.

It's time for me to act. With adrenaline pumping through my veins, I emerge from my hiding spot and sprint up the footpath towards him. I put my hand in my pocket, feeling for my Taser.

Paul seems to hear the sound of my boots because he begins to spin. However, I'm already on him before he can do anything, I snatch the

Taser from my pocket, slam it into his neck and press the trigger. The impact is otherworldly. Paul didn't just jerk, he literally convulsed before he hit the floor. Panicked that I must have killed him, I check his pulse and breathe easy when I feel something on my fingers.

I drag Paul's limp body into the darkened house. This phase of the plan demands a lot of detail, so I set about putting everything in place.

I secure Paul in a chair with rolls of duct tape tightly wrapped around his torso and limbs, rendering him immobile. As I work, Paul begins to stir, but I pay him no mind.

I retrieve supplies from my car and carefully set up the next phase. Peering out the window before making my way back to the car, I cautiously reverse into the driveway next to Paul's vehicle. Slowly, I unload items from my car and carry them into the house, making multiple trips until everything is inside.

Locking all doors behind me, I discard my jacket and approach the boxes I brought in. Kneeling down, I slip on a pair of gloves and open one of the containers. Inside lies a 12-gauge shotgun and several boxes of ammunition. Without hesitation, I lift the weapon and grab the ammo.

In another compartment rests an H&K 416C assault rifle along with cartridges. My fingers tighten around the weapon as I peer through its Aimpoint sight. A box filled with hundreds of rounds catches my eye in the corner, ready to be used.

I carefully place the loaded guns back into their boxes and hoist them onto my shoulder. My footsteps are light as I make my way over to Paul, who is slowly regaining consciousness. He blinks repeatedly, trying to focus his eyes as I set the boxes down behind him. From one of the bags I had brought in earlier, I retrieve some fishing line and get right to work.

I skilfully attach the loaded shotgun to Paul's right arm, securing it with strips of duct tape. Making sure his finger is positioned next to the trigger, I neatly wrap the thin line around his finger and stretch it towards the entrance door handle. With precise movements, I tie off the line and step back to admire my handiwork.

My plan is simple but effective – when someone attempts to enter through the door, the pulling down on the handle will cause Paul's finger to pull the trigger.

That done, I take the H&K assault rifle and the boxes of ammo to the window facing the driveway. It's boarded up, so I crack it open a little. Loading a fresh magazine into the rifle, I calmly keep it on the window sill, the muzzle peeking out a little, and then I peer through the red dot as I scan the street, noting areas where I will be taking my shots. Perfect. I pull my eyes from the sight system and smile a little at what I've done.

So far, so good. Everything is going as planned.

Paul has started mumbling sounds behind me now. I sigh. Even at a time like this, he doesn't know when to stop talking. I ignore him. Taking one final look around, happy with my work.

I pick up my phone from a stack of boxes in the corner of the room and dial 999. A woman answers me a few seconds later. "Hello, emergency services operator. Which services do you require? Fire, police or ambulance?"

"Police," I answer.

"I'll put you through," the voice on the other end says.

"All of our emergency operators are on another call at the moment, someone will be with you shortly." Are you fucking kidding me!! I'm on hold to the police? No wonder people don't like us.

"Hello, police. How can I help?"

Time for an Oscar-winning performance. "This is Detective Nicole Murphy. I've been kidnapped by my partner Paul Adams. He ran from the station this morning after he was detained regarding the recent murders. There should be a BOLO on the system for him," I say.

I can hear her tapping her keyboard.

"Where are you, ma'am?" There is now a slight urgency in her voice.

"You have to hurry up, please send help. He's . . . He's coming. I was able to hide, but I can hear him downstairs. I'm hiding in a wardrobe, but I think he's going to find me..."

"Please calm down, Detective Murphy," the woman's voice is gentle and kind. "Just tell me where you are, and I'll get the police right there to you."

I don't answer, but my rapid breathing speaks volumes.

"Detective, you need to calm down and tell me where you are. If you don't know where, I need you to check. That is the only way we can get to you and help."

"Have the tech team trace my location using my phone number. I don't know how long I can stay on line talking to you." I took the block I had on my phone off before making the call so I know that they will be able to pick up our location within minutes.

"Please hurry, he seems very unstable."

"Don't worry, Detective. I've notified the tech team, and they should be getting your location within the next few minutes. Please find some safe place to hide, and we will be there soon."

"Okay, please ..." I don't finish and hang up the call.

That was splendid acting, if I do say so myself.

Ignoring Paul's muffled voice, I return my eyes to the H&K Aimpoint CompM4 red dot system and then wait.

Help should be around the corner soon.

Chapter Thirty-One

CHECKMATE

Paul

Is this how I am going to die? Is this the end of me, taped to a chair with a shotgun on my right arm? It's a rhetorical question because I know, without a doubt, I'm going to die. I should have known better. Again, I berate myself for being too dim-witted in this kind of thing. Nicole has played me again. I should have known she was never going to let me live. Should have known it's going to come down to this.

I know what she's doing. All of it. Once I'd awoken and I felt the gag in my mouth and then saw the shotgun on my right hand, I knew instantly what she had planned.

Death by firing squad.

I look around where we are, and there's a number of weapons and boxes of ammunition laid around.

She walks past me, holding an assault rifle.

Is that an H&K? I don't see much through the haze, and I try and blink it away, but I know it is.

On a holiday a few years ago to the States, my friend Gus, who is a fan of American-made rifles, had shown me his collection and take me to a shooting range. We got to handle lots of different types and learn the history behind them. Just from that memory, I can see that there are M4 carbines, AR-15s, a few Glocks, and some I don't recognise.

Nicole is calmly walking around the room as she sets up her scene. I can't let this happen. I need to stop this. But my voice is not audible through the gag. I have to speak sense into her.

Nicole hears my inaudible mutterings, she glances at me and continues setting up. I guess she's way past talking to me now. God, I can't let her hurt anyone else. She moves over to the window, which has a few boxes placed in front of it, and she balances the rifle on its tripod and points the barrel out of a gap in the wooden boards.

She picks up her phone from the boxes and dials a number.

What is she doing?

Looking dead at me, she makes a panicked call. Her voice sounds scared and panicked. I can't make out everything she's saying, but I can guess that it's not good. She finishes the call, putting the phone back in her pocket, and kneels down to look through the scope of the rifle as she moves it around, placing it to her liking.

I struggle with my binds, but it's of no use. I can't move or talk. All I can do is sit and watch.

Soon I hear cars pulling up and several doors closing.

Next thing I know, Nicole starts firing thousands of rounds; the sound is deafening. When she's exhausted the mag, she's quick to reload and opens fire again. From where I am, I can't see if she has hit anyone. How many are dead or hurt? I have no idea. When will this stop? The mag expends again, and she slams in another one and empties this one just as quickly as the last one. When this magazine exhausts itself, she doesn't reload, rather she pulls the rifle out of the window and, in a crouch, quickly moves further back in the room.

Everywhere is silent. And then I hear the thud of footsteps outside. The cops are coming to the door. I glance at the shotgun taped on my right arm and notice the fishing wire wrapped around my finger and extended to the door handle. Oh, God. No! I shout, "Don't come in!

Don't come in! It's a trap." But my voice is muffled. That doesn't matter, though. I see the door handle swinging down and then the door itself being pulled back.

Like a puppet on a string, the line draws my finger back, and it presses the trigger. Boom! I involuntarily fire a shot at the door. Hundreds of ball bearings flying in a scattered formation slam into the wooden surface of the door and crack it. I hear a grunt and someone falling, I've hit someone; I don't know if it's critical or not.

It doesn't matter, anyway, because I know what's going to happen next.

Beads of sweat drip down my forehead as I brace myself for the impending impact. Gunfire erupts from all angles, an onslaught of destruction that splinters furniture and shatters glass. Bullets rake through my body, slamming into my chest, stomach, arms, and legs with merciless force. My muscles spasm and contort as if being electrocuted.

The chair beneath finally gives way and falls back, but I barely register the pain as adrenaline floods my system. I am dying.

The gunfire ceases suddenly, and I can only assume the cops are reloading. My vision blurs as I struggle to stay conscious, feeling blood pooling around me and realising I've vomited and pissed on myself.

Through a hazy fog, I see a figure approach me – Nicole. Her face is framed by a lock of wild hair, holding a pair of scissors.

She quickly cuts through the duct tape binding me and removes the gag from my mouth. My attempts to speak result in only guttural sounds and bloody bubbles escaping my lips. But it doesn't matter because I know I am already dead. As she finishes freeing me, she slips back into the shadows of the room just before the cops burst through the door.

Her final move... checkmate.

It's perfect.

How she thought of all of this, I have no idea, and to be quite honest, I'm not going to allow her to be the last thought I have on this earth. Instead, I think of happier times. My childhood, the feeling of the sun on my face on a nice summer's day... It's starting not to hurt anymore.

All the noise in my head is slowly fading away finally... silence.

Chapter Thirty-Two

CURTAIN CALL

Nicole

Hmm. Nothing is more comforting than a wool blanket wrapped around you on a chilly summer morning. I'm in the back of one of the ambulances that was called to the scene, an IV bag beside me, and its fluid injected into my skin. Paramedics who'd hovered around me earlier are smart and intelligent enough to know I wasn't hurt in any way, but they still need to give me something. Always err on the side of precaution, I guess.

And I agree, well, for this instance.

As soon as I'd pulled the duct tape from Paul after the fusillade of bullets from the police impacted the whole room and poor Paul, I'd gone straight to the rear of the house, carrying a shovel I'd picked up from a small shed on the northeastern side of the house. I ran the length of the 100-metre garden and started digging. I knew that all I would have was exactly 90 seconds before the police entered the house to find Paul's mangled body and then start their search of the rest of the house. I need to be in my hiding spot so as not to destroy my story.

I do a fast work on the digging. Not deep and not exactly shallow. And then I dump the tapes, guns, and the burner phone. I closed it back with the shovel and started racing back to the house.

When I enter through the back door, I hear the sound of footsteps and hushed tones in the entrance hall; they're already inside, impressive. I'd told the lady on the emergency line that I had hidden myself, so I search for someplace in the house to hide. I find it soon enough. An empty wardrobe near the master bedroom. I don't have to wait more than a few minutes before I hear voices, and then I see the beams of light from their flashlights. The doors open, and a handsome officer greets me and then offers a hand.

I grasp it, and he helps me out.

Five minutes with the paramedics and two police detectives come by to chat with me. My story is straight and fully backed up. I tell them everything. I make it a bit fuzzy, just to sound believable, considering Paul, the serial killer, had somehow drugged me when I entered my flat and then had gotten me here while I was still unconscious. The detectives nod at this and ask a few more questions again, and then they tell me that I may have to come down to the station to give a statement blah, blah, blah. I'm no longer listening.

My mission is done, and I just want to rest.

But the coroner was waiting to move Paul's body from the house into their van. Damn medical teams. I mean, can't they just drive me to a hospital and deal with his body later. I watch as the cops mill in and out of the house, talking to each other, the detectives scratching their heads, trying to figure out how one of their colleagues, one of their friends, could have been caught up in something so horrible.

The quicker they get over this and lay the case to rest, the better it is for everyone.

It takes the coroner 15 minutes to zip up Paul's body and load him on a stretcher before bringing him out to the van. I listen to them talk as they load him into the van and lock the stretcher in place. The paramedic seeing to me helps me to my feet and inside the ambulance and then slowly lays me down on the stretcher. I close my eyes, hear the doors close, then feel the ambulance start to move.

When I wake up, I'm in the hospital. I'm on the bed with hospital sheets around me. My head is groggy, and my vision is blurry.

It takes me a second to realise that the nurses sedated me. Seriously. I said I was fine. They knew I was fine. Then why this? God! This sucks. Now I know how my victims felt. Karma.

I lean back in bed and let everything that's happened over the last few weeks flow over me.

Paul is dead, and I'm alive. He's the serial killer that has had the city in a choke hold, and I'm just an innocent woman. For the rest of history, he will be remembered for his acts of violence, not for his fortitude. I realise I'm already smiling. I hear footsteps outside and soon see Pangborn himself walk into the room. He has a bunch of flowers in his right hand, roses. Hmm. I fight not to roll my eyes.

He comes to my side and puts the roses on the bedside table. He looks me over and says, "Sorry we didn't put security in place for you or your mother sooner. We should have done better to protect you and your family."

"It's not your fault…"

Pangborn shakes his head. "No, it is… I should have known as partners, he's going to target you. We should have kept someone watching over you."

And I'd have killed him or her. I sigh and say, "He would have killed them to get to me, and I wouldn't want to have more people's deaths on my head. I already have to deal with the fact that he was able to get to my mother for the rest of my life."

Pangborn thinks this over a moment. Then he says, "You're right. I'm so sorry that your mother got dragged into this… It's hard to believe that someone like that, someone so evil, was hidden under our noses all this time, I still can't believe it. . ." He struggles for words.

"It's crazy," I say looking at him. He looks tired and sad.

"Yeah," he says, nodding, his eyes reflecting his far-off thoughts. Recollecting himself, he clears his throat and says, "The doctors told me you'll be out tomorrow."

Shit. I know where this is going, and I don't like it, not one bit. Still, I say, "Yes. I'm not hurt. But they just pumped me with liquids to counteract anything he could have given me."

Pangborn nods. "Good... I want you to take some time off before coming back to the station."

I try to speak, but he waves me off.

He says, "What you've been through isn't just anything. You may think it's nothing, but I assure you, you need to take some time off, get your head together. Go on holiday or something. I want you feeling your best before you come back to work full time. I want you to make sure that you get your head right..."

"Sir, are you indirectly asking me to see a shrink?"

Pangborn nods. "Yes. I am."

I try not to roll my eyes again.

Pangborn sighs and then starts walking out of the room. He stops almost to the door and turns to me, saying, "Try and see that you do that, Nicole. It's for your own good. Trust me."

"I will, sir," I say. Can you go now, please?

He nods once at me and walks out of the door.

I'm discharged the following day without much fanfare, thank God. The last thing I need is the whole of the station to be out there holding out flowers and wishing me well. Ugh!

"Thanks," I say to the nurse who helps me outside. As expected, Pangborn is waiting for me with his grey Mini in the car park. Are you really going to keep on doing this? I think but I don't say.

I'm assuming he sees something in me now, his star detective. Mix that in with a shit ton of guilt, and he's more than likely going to be like this for a while.

With a smiling face, he opens the door for me and helps me into the car. As he drives me home, he makes a joke that I shouldn't expect him to be my chauffeur for much longer. Thank you, Jeesuus! I smile and tell him he's done enough already. It's one of those hypocritical answers that I hate, but oh well. When he drops me off at home, he helps me up the front stairs and to my flat door. I insistently tell him I'm fine – men and their forced chivalry, but I'm a great pretender, and I just let him. He tells me to remember to call the therapist and book an appointment and that he will be checking to make sure that I do.

I just nod to this. Whatever you say, boss. I physically tip an imaginary hat at him as he leaves.

Chapter Thirty-Three

NICE TALKING TO YOU

Nicole

So, that's my story. Some may consider it a confession, but let me make one thing clear: I have no remorse or guilt for anything I've said. In fact, I feel the opposite. This was just a way to pass the time.

But there is one thing that does gnaw at me. Paul. I regret that our relationship had to end in such a messy and violent way. However, I must give credit where credit is due. He has inspired my next artistic phase, and let me tell you, it will be nothing short of brilliant.

I wish you could see the look on your face right now – pure confusion. It's hilarious, really. And honestly, I don't care what you do after this. You can sit and wonder if I told the truth or just made up an elaborate tale. You could even go report me to the police, but how would you know that you're not speaking to me?

Anyway, it's been nice talking to you. Who knows, maybe we will end up running into each other again sometime... By the way, you have really pretty eyes.

THE END

Epilogue

It's been eight months since everything went down. I went back to work for a few months. It did take a while to get back into the swing of things, and that's only because, for the first few months, I had everyone hovering over me like I was going to have some sort of meltdown at any point. I was placed on desk duty so that I wouldn't have to deal with potential PTSD from attending any crime scenes.

Pangborn assigned me only basic cases; his way of trying to protect me. I assured him it wasn't necessary, but he paid no attention to my protests. It drove me crazy. But what was even more maddening were the constant calls and emails from news agencies vying for an exclusive interview. Some studios even approached me about turning my story into a Lifetime or Netflix top 10 movie. Despite some tempting six-figure offers, my answer stayed the same: "I'm going to have to decline. I want to move on and not relive any of the horrific events that took place."

Fortunately, I don't need the money or fame. With my mother's recent passing and inheriting her and my father's estate, including selling our family home, I am now set for life... twice over, in fact.

After much consideration, I've come to the conclusion that I need a change of scenery. London is also no longer safe for me to continue my little hobby.

When thinking of where to move to, the most important detail was where I could go that would allow me to blend in? I, of course, will change my identity and have all my papers in order.

It then came to me while I was flicking through TV channels... Yes. Now it might seem weird, moving to one of the most glamorous cities in the world, where everyone wants to be seen and everyone knows their name, but for me, it's the perfect place to disappear among the crowd. It's actually fantastic, now that I think about it. The perfect place for me to showcase my new era.

This is going to be fun...